AMERICAN D-BOY II

THE RETURN OF D-BOY

AMERICAN D-BOY
BOOK 2

BILLIGOAT

WAHIDA CLARK'S
INNOVATIVE PUBLISHING

Wahida Clark Presents Publishing

75 Washington St, Unit 383

Fairburn GA, 30213

1(866)910-6920

www.wclarkpublishing.com

American D-Boy Part 1

ISBN 13-digit 978-1-957954-48-6 (Paper)

ISBN 13-digit 978-1-957954-47-9 (Hardback)

ISBN 13-digit 978-1-957954-49-3 (eBook)

1. New York- 3. Drug Trafficking- 4. African American-

Fiction- 5. Urban Fiction- 6. Street gangs- 7. D-Boy

Cover design and layout by Nuance Art, LLC

Book design by NuanceArt

www.NuanceArtLLc.com

Printed in USA

PROLOGUE: THE RETURN OF D-BOY

HOT 104 RADIO STATION NEW YORK CITY

THERE WAS a somber mood at the radio station. Today marked a year since D-Boy's demise. His only brother, Jay-Roc, was keeping it together for his family and the successful team they created before D-Boy's early departure. D-Boy and Jay-Roc built the American D-Boy brand into a multi-million-dollar empire in just two years. They created a record label with platinum artists, and a lucrative clothing line all named after the owner and record label, American D-Boy.

Just when the American D-Boy brand was glowing-up, D-Boy was killed from a car bomb that exploded from the inside of the car. He was blown to bits; his body was literally obliterated into a million pieces then scorched from the fire. There were no remains that could be used as physical material that resembled a body.

"Burying my brothers' remains was the hardest thing I ever had to do in my life," Jay-Roc said into the studio microphone.

"I can't imagine what you went through because I'm the only child, so I definitely can't relate." DJ Red Zone paused before

1

speaking again, "This next song is dedicated to the memory of D-Boy. You'll never be forgotten."

"Long Live D-Boy," Jay-Roc said to conclude the interview.

Everyone sat silently as the song played. When it was over the executive producer gave DJ Red Zone the sign to end the show.

"That's a wrap!" DJ Red Zone announced. He stood up and approached Jay-Roc with a brotherly handshake and a hug. "Thank you for coming down today."

"Don't mention it. I'm always willing to help a fellow DJ," Jay-Roc responded solemnly.

At that moment Jay-Roc's phone rang. "Excuse me I have to take this call." Jay-Roc started walking away so no one was within earshot of his call.

"I heard you on the radio acting like a little bitch over my death," D-Boy said playfully.

"Fuck you bro', I did my best to fake that shit." Jay-Roc smiled. "What are you going to do now?"

"Me and my lawyer, John, are in this shit together." D-Boy took a deep breath. "We are going to Dubai to relax and have some fun. After all this drama, all I need is a long vacation."

"Are you planning on coming back?" Jay-Roc asked hesitantly.

"John said after seven years we should be able to sneak back in with different identities." D-Boy looked across the room at John before continuing, "John said the statute of limitations on mysterious deaths is seven years. So, expect me in exactly six more years, big brother."

"That's a bet." Jay-Roc got a lump in his throat. "I'm going to miss you, little brother."

"*I'm going to miss you little brother*,'" D-Boy said in an imitation of a female's voice. "You sound like a little bitch."

"Fuck you, D-Boy!"

"You know I'm just fucking with you. I'm going to miss you and Grandpa Joe's crazy ass."

Jay-Roc was one of the three people who knew the truth about D-Boy faking his death. The CIA was either going to kill him or have him locked up forever. The plan to fake his death was the brainchild of his lawyer, John Gillespie. John faked his own death, too, because the CIA knew he was onto them.

"I love you, big bro'." D-Boy got a lump in his throat.

"I love you, too, lil' bro'." Jay-Roc's eyes watered up, but he wouldn't let the tears fall.

"I'll see you in six more years." D-Boy hung up and headed for a private jet landing in Dubai.

CHAPTER 1
SIX YEARS LATER...

HOT 104 RADIO STATION, NEW YORK CITY

THE HOT 104 radio station was packed to the max. There were cameras flashing while onlookers gawked at the three stunning males standing before them. They were in a rap group called the Billigoats and the hottest rap group alive. Their debut album, titled *Billionaire Goats,* did three billion streams in its first month, making them the first rap group in history to have a debut album streamed over a billion times in a month.

The trio consisted of Mouf, Prime the God, and Dirty Redd. Each of the members wore diamond encrusted white gold Cuban link chains with huge custom made American D-Boy Records medallions, also encrusted with diamonds. Each member had diamond watches, rings, and bracelets to go with the chains.

Each of the members were draped in custom made Billigoat Classic Collection apparel. It was a clothing line Dirty Redd designed that ended up being the group's namesake. They followed the successful blueprint of the American D-Boy clothing line and record label combination. The Billigoat clothing line began to sell out in clothing stores everywhere. Although Dirty Redd designed it, each member had a stake in the company.

They gazed out into the crowd and smiled as the people held up their cell phones to record them live. The flashlights from all the phones looked like mini stars directed at the three men. They were relishing the moment because today they were making a major announcement.

"Okay people, quiet down! We have a major announcement to make," said Mouf as the crowd immediately adhered to his demand. "We are leaving the states to record our entire sophomore album in Dubai. And we're headlining a world tour starting in Dubai."

A redhead female reporter with large horn-rimmed glasses raised her hand so she could speak. Out of all the reporters in attendance she was the most aggressive. Prime could not help but notice her. You could see her piercing ice blue eyes through the lens, giving her an air of exotic beauty.

"Get shorty over there with the red hair," Prime whispered to Mouf.

"We'll start with you over there." Mouf pointed his finger toward the redhead woman.

"My name is Gina Franklin from Hip-Hop Daily. How long will you be in Dubai? And, when the album is finished will there be release parties in the US? Finally, is there going to be a tribute to the late great D-Boy, creator, and founder of American D-Boy Records?"

"I'm going to let the boss man answer that one. Without Jay-Roc none of this would be possible. Come on up, Roc, and answer some of these important questions," Mouf said with a huge smile, knowing that Jay-Roc hated to speak in public.

Jay-Roc also hated to answer questions pertaining to his brother D-Boy. There was a lot of speculation about his untimely demise. Jay-Roc stepped up from behind the three men. "How you all doing? We will be in Dubai for about three months. That includes recording and touring. And yes, we will be turning up in America when the album is done! We cannot forget America. The name of our label is American D-Boy, so you know we're going to do it big in the US."

Jay-Roc smiled before continuing, "To answer your last question Miss Franklin, we haven't thought about it but now that you mention it, we will put together a tribute song for my brother D-Boy." He rescinded back to his perch behind the trio.

"We leave tomorrow morning for Dubai, however, we will be throwing a going away party at the Ritz Carleton where we'll be performing," Prime commented. "Be there or be square."

"Word!" Dirty Redd chimed in. "So make sure you are there, you do not want to miss this. I promise you!" Dirty Redd kissed his fist and made a peace sign. "See you soon!"

"Thank you for coming down. We'll see you tonight," Mouf closed out and the trio headed for the exit, escorted by three security guards to a black SUV.

After everyone got settled into the vehicle, Jay-Roc spoke. "Listen, this is going to be the biggest move in your career thus far. The United Arab Emirates is where all the money is at, and we are going to get a lot of it while we're there." He paused to give them a serious look. "Don't fuck this up! Do not, I repeat, *do not* go over there with that American street mentality. They will make an example out of you, so please be on your best behavior."

"We got you, Roc," Prime said, speaking on behalf of the collective.

"Word, Roc, you made it happen for us. I'm not trying to fuck this up and be back on the street hustling," Dirty Redd said with confidence.

"We're going to make you proud, facts!" Mouf ended the pact with Roc.

"I'm going to jump in the Wraith. I'll meet you guys later

7

tonight at the Ritz." Jay-Roc exited the vehicle and got into his jet-black Rolls Royce.

Jay-Roc watched as the SUV drove off before taking a phone from the glove compartment and making a call. It rang twice before it was answered. "What's popping big bro'! It has been a while since you called my line. Is everything okay?" D-Boy asked.

"Yeah, everything's fine. I just called to tell you I am coming to Dubai to see you. I'm bringing Tracy and Lil' D-Boy with me."

"You can't come here! You'll blow my cover for sure. The FEDS already think something was fishy. I don't need them following you here to pin my whereabouts," D-Boy spoke with aggression to prove his point. "Besides that, I'm coming to America. The seven years is up."

"I know. Relax little brother, I got this," Jay-Roc responded nonchalantly. "I just had a major press conference at Hot 104 announcing big news that the Billigoats are recording their sophomore album exclusively in Dubai. We are also doing a world tour starting in Dubai. So, believe me I have my bases covered."

D-Boy was put at ease from the elaborate planning Jay-Roc put into this trip. "Okay, big bro', you got it all covered. When are you coming to Dubai?"

"Tomorrow."

"What!" D-Boy was excited and bewildered at the same time. "You didn't even give me a chance to put together some outings. It's a lot of fun stuff to do over here."

"Well, you'll have plenty of time to show us around and to bond with your nephew, Lil' D-Boy, that you never met," Jay-Roc reminded D-Boy about his nephew.

"You're right, big bro', I've never laid eyes on my nephew, my namesake. Lil' D-Boy." D-Boy smiled because he didn't have a little D-Boy of his own. "I'm looking forward to meeting

Lil' D-Boy and seeing my big brother. I miss you, shit, it's been seven years."

"I know time is flying. Lil' D-Boy is already six years old in the first grade. He always looks at your picture and says 'D-Boy, Daddy! Big D-Boy'."

"Wow! So, he knows my face." This intrigued D-Boy.

"It's like he knows you because since he was one, he would stop and stare at your picture for hours at a time. He's always been fascinated with you," Jay-Roc said with a smile.

"When I see him tomorrow, I'm going to spoil him the right way, the D-Boy way." D-Boy smiled at the thought of being able to spend time with his nephew.

"Alright, lil' bro', I'll see you tomorrow in Dubai. Love you, bro'." Jay-Roc smiled before hanging up.

———

BUREAU OF SPECIAL INVESTIGATION, ABU DUBAI, UNITED ARAB EMIRATES

Special Agents Ali Bashar and Malik Mohammed were sitting at a desk when they got a call about a rich American Black man that was spending so much money they thought he was royalty. Upon investigating the man, they discovered that he had no job, but he'd spent on average $100K a year for the last six years. They were gathering intel on his day-to-day schedule and who he communicated with.

From what they could gather, he was pretty much a loaner. He had one friend who lived with him. They both stayed to themselves. The occasional prostitute visiting the two was all the company they had. As they followed him, they didn't notice anything peculiar until today. Something about the conversation led them to believe there was something deeper about this man than meets the eye.

"Did you get all of that?" Agent Bashar asked his partner who was already contemplating the conversation.

"Not really, it was kind of muffled." Agent Mohammed squinted his eyes and rubbed his forehead. "I think we should contact the American FBI to coordinate this investigation with them."

"Let's wait and gather more intel. You know how those American agents can get arrogant with us because they think they're better at law enforcement than anyone," Agent Mohammed said from experience working with American agents.

"I agree with you on that, I can't stand those infidels," Agent Bashar stated with venom in his tone. "Besides, if we get them in on it, they'll take credit for any big arrest. Why make them the hero when we can be the agents that save the day?"

"Exactly my point!" Agent Mohammed raised his voice with excitement, "This could be our big break in law enforcement. Let's keep this to ourselves for now, not even our captain needs to know yet. I got a feeling we may be on to something big."

The two men looked at one another with a serious look that sealed their agreement. Agent Bashar stuck out his hand to receive a brotherly shake that would consummate their deal. Agent Mohammed obliged by grabbing his hand and gripping it tight to show loyalty.

They both stared at the pictures they privately took of the man that were pinned to a bulletin board. They had thoughts of who he really was, and what he was hiding from the American FEDS. They were good at conjuring up what could be, but they had no idea who they were really dealing with.

———

THE RITZ-CARLTON, **NEW YORK CITY**

The hotel room was extravagant, with marble floors and

countertops and pristine white walls with a balcony overlooking the immaculate New York City skyline. The only problem with the room was the Billigoats had somewhat of an afterparty there. The whole room was filled with naked exotic women, so there were clothes flung all around the suite. There were about ten women total, three women for each man with one left over.

When Jay-Roc entered the room with the bodyguard in tow, he could not believe his eyes. He took out his phone and turned on his loud alarm. "Get the fuck up! Let's go! We have a six-thirty a.m. flight to Dubai." He marched around the suite, making as much noise as he could muster. "Let's go, damnit!"

Mouf was the first to open his eyes. "What the fuck?" he asked half woke, reeking of alcohol and weed. "What time is it?"

"It's time to get up," Jay-Roc replied. "You have fifteen minutes to get up and ready to board a private jet to Dubai. Unless you are trying to miss the flight and mess up the best opportunity of your lives, I suggest you get up and wake up your buddies. I'll be waiting in the sprinter. Fifteen minutes!" Jay-Roc and the bodyguard exited the room.

Mouf got into action waking up and quickly getting dressed. He saw Dirty Redd. "Bro' get up! Jay-Roc just came in and said if we're not ready in fifteen minutes we're fucked!"

"What time is it?" Dirty Redd asked with a groggy throat. "We just went to sleep like an hour ago." He fought to get himself up but lost because he just laid there and fell back asleep.

"Where's Prime?" Mouf searched the suite with no sign of Prime. He began to panic. "Yo, where the fuck is Prime? I don't see him anywhere."

He kept searching then remembered there was one place he didn't look and that was the bathroom. He entered the spacious bathroom and there was Prime in the tub with two women knocked out.

Mouf approached him and shook his shoulder. "Prime we

have to go! Jay-Roc is waiting for us in the sprinter. If we don't get there in the next ten minutes, we're done, bro'! Let's go!"

Prime looked at his Rolex. "Oh shit! Our flight leaves at six-thirty and it's five-fifteen!" Prime jumped up leaving the two women to slump over onto each other because he was their pillar.

Mouf and Prime were both up and putting on their sneakers. Dirty Redd was the only one still sleeping. All the women were slowly getting up and getting dressed. One of the women started cleaning up the room throwing liquor bottles in the garbage.

"Bro', get your ass up!" Mouf half-shouted. "Why you always the one that be slow poking all the time?"

"Fuck you mean? I'm getting up, don't rush me!" Dirty Redd knew it was true, he was the slow poke of the crew.

Everyone proceeded to leave the room. Dirty Redd was still putting on his sneakers. They moved like a huge entourage through the extravagant hotel lobby headed to the parking garage where the sprinter was waiting.

When they reached the sprinter, one of the girls grabbed Mouf by the arm. "Don't be a stranger. You know my IG name, hit my inbox." She was gorgeous and voluptuous.

"No, you hit my inbox." Mouf nicely removed her hand from his arm. "Now if you'll excuse me, I have a flight to catch." He entered the sprinter while she pouted in disbelief.

Four of the other girls tried to get into the sprinter. "I don't know where you think you're going, but it is mos def not on this sprinter," Prime said aggressively while smiling. "We had a great time, and you all are baddies! But Dubai is waiting."

"Come on, Prime, it's—" she shouted.

Prime shut the door while she was talking. "Enough of that." Prime reached his hand out to Jay-Roc. "What's up, boss man?"

After giving Prime a firm handshake, he looked around the spacious sprinter, bewildered. "Where the fuck is Dirty Redd?"

12

Jay-Roc asked in a strange tone. "Like really, he's doing this shit again! He's always the last one for everything."

As Jay-Roc spoke, Dirty Redd was approaching the sprinter at a lite jog. "I'm coming!" he yelled as the vehicle began to drive before abruptly stopping. "Damn, you were going to leave me!" Dirty Redd said while panting from the jog.

"Get your chubby ass in the van!" Prime said, joking about his weight, as he assisted him with getting into the vehicle.

"Nice of you to make it," Jay-Roc said while giving him a brotherly handshake and a smile.

"I wouldn't miss this for the world," Dirty Redd replied while breathing heavily.

As the sprinter drove off, no one noticed the redhead girl from the press conference sitting in a gray Nissan Sentra. She quickly started the car and began to follow them. She was very discreet. She had been shadowing them for a year now. She made sure she stayed at a distance so she would not trip any suspicion. She was a professional, possibly the best female spy agent in the field.

She dialed a contact in her phone. "This is Special Agent code name Sparrow. I am trailing suspects to the private jet now. It's confirmed they are going to Dubai for the duration of three months."

"Okay great. We will have one of our jets waiting for you at the same location. You will be flying out twenty minutes after them to the same airport in Dubai. We will create a delay, so you will land before them. Make sure you get a visual on the big brother, Jay -Roc. He is the key."

"Copy."

"When you land in Dubai, you'll be given further instructions." Special Agent George Heron hung up the phone.

"I can't wait to see you alive. It'll be like seeing a ghost. The ghost of D-Boy." He leaned back in his chair and took a pull of his cigar while gazing out of the window at his illustrious property.

CHAPTER 2
DUBAI INTERNATIONAL AIRPORT

Jay-Roc purchased the Cessna Citation X, one of the fastest Private Jets a civilian could own. They were able to travel at twice the speed of commercial airlines. The average flight time on a commercial flight from New York to Dubai is twelve hours and forty-five minutes. In the Cessna they would touchdown in Dubai in exactly six hours and twenty-three minutes flat.

"If you look to your left, you'll see the Burj Khalifa, the tallest tower in the world," the pilot announced over the PA system like a professional tour guide.

"Wow!" Mouf said while looking out of the jet's window at the Dubai skyline. "It's not as lit as the New York City skyline, but dam near close."

"Word! That shit is beautiful." Dirty Redd took out his cell phone. "I have to take pics of this for my fans."

Prime and Jay-Roc were both napping while the jet was preparing for a landing. Tracy and Lil' D-Boy were resting as well but they all woke up when the pilot made another announcement, "Please put on your seatbelts and prepare for landing."

"Are we here yet, Daddy?" Lil' D-Boy asked.

"Yes son, we are officially in Dubai, and you're finally going to meet—" Jay-Roc cut himself off mid-sentence. *I almost let the cat out of the bag. They cannot know that my brother is alive for their own safety. We all can go down for aiding and abetting a fugitive of the United States.*

"What you say, Daddy?" Lil' D-Boy was confused because he was very smart, so he knew something was strange.

"Nothing, you're finally going to meet Daddy's good friend from Dubai. He's so close to me that I consider him a brother, so you can call him Uncle," Jay-Roc said while glancing at Tracy. She was the only one besides Jay-Roc that knew the truth about D-Boy.

The jet taxied and everyone exited the jet to be met on the tarmac by a white Rolls Royce Cullinan and a driver. The driver wore traditional Arab garb, and he had a big beard and dark designer Gucci aviator glasses. When he saw them getting off, he directed them toward the Cullinan.

"This way my friends," he spoke with a thick Arab accent. "Welcome to Dubai, I'm Mustafa, your personal driver and guide. Anything you need just let Mustafa know and your wish is my command."

"Cool! Like our own personal genie," Dirty Redd said with mock sarcasm. "All I want is some good food and maybe one of those bad ass Dubai chicks to keep me company."

"Here you go," Mouf said. "We just touched down and you already trying to get hitched out here. You know you're a sucker for love, don't get caught up out here."

"Whatever your heart desires. If it is a- how you say, a bad Dubai woman. Then you will have the best of the best," Mustafa assured.

"That's what's up! While you're at it get me one, too. The best of the best sounds good to me," Prime concurred.

"You got it brother," Mustafa replied.

"All I want is to get to work. I got some fire ideas for some music," Mouf said.

"Oh yes, I can take you to the suite where the studio is," Mustafa said.

"So, we have a studio in the suite where we'll be staying?" asked Prime.

"Yes sir, everything is in the suite, so you don't have to go anywhere to record." Mustafa smiled. "And might I add, it's the latest in state-of-the-art recording equipment."

They put all the luggage in the vehicle, and they all piled into the luxury SUV. They headed toward the Bulgari Resort, one of the most prestigious resorts in the world. Jay-Roc didn't spare any money on this trip. He knew that this was more than just a trip, to him it was a reuniting with his only sibling, D-Boy.

———

THE SPARROW WAS ABOUT fifty yards from her suspects watching them from the driver's seat of a black Alpha Romeo Giulia. She landed about thirty minutes before them. She got her instructions and all she had to do now was wait.

"They landed and are now on the move."

"Good. Stay on them and don't blow your cover because they saw you at the press conference," Agent Heron said.

"Understood. I have one of my many disguises on, so it'll be hard for them to pin me."

"I may have you engage in a 'Honey Trap' with one of the group members so you can be in the inner circle and get better intel."

"Whatever you want me to do. I think that's a better plan because It's almost impossible to get intel like this," she responded.

"From your knowledge which one of the members is most likely to fall for you romantically?"

"That's an easy one. The one they call Dirty Redd."

"Explain."

"Well, he's the only one that has had sexual relationships with Caucasian women. And I believe he is the most vulnerable emotionally because I observed him crying over a woman six months ago. I can take advantage of his emotions and manipulate them to my bidding," Sparrow said nonchalantly.

"I couldn't have planned it better myself. Let me know when the 'Honey Trap' is successful. If there are any changes, I'll contact you. Other than that, keep up the good work, Special Agent Sparrow."

Special Agent Sparrow was a loaner with no family or friends. She was inducted into the CIA because of a drug overdose. The CIA often recruit junkies and prostitutes because they are easy to control and easy to exterminate. While she was in the hospital recovering, she was approached by Special Agent Heron and given an offer that would change her life forever. She thought back to that fateful day six years ago:

"Where am I?" She tried to move but her wrist was chained to the bed.

"Relax," Agent Heron said. "You are in Bellevue Hospital recovering from an overdose of heroin. You're chained to the bed because we need answers as to where you got heroin this strong." He knew the answer to that question. He was the one that supplied the dealer that served her. He was covering his tracks.

She thought to herself before asking, "Wait a minute what happened to Jessica, Tony, Mike, and Sharon?" Those were her junky buddies.

Agent Heron took a deep breath. "They're all dead. They didn't survive the overdose, you are the only survivor," he paused to let it sink in before continuing, "The heroin you all shot up was laced with Fentanyl. The doctors said you had such a high tolerance that the Fentanyl didn't kill you, it just rendered you unconscious."

Agent Heron knew how the deadly drug Fentanyl was getting into the country, too.

She began to weep hysterically, "No! This can't be true! I want out of here now!" She struggled to free her wrist from the cuff to no avail.

"I'm sorry but you can't leave until you answer some questions," Agent Heron said.

"I don't have to answer shit! I didn't commit a crime so take these fucking cuffs off me, now!" She was seething with anger.

Agent Heron smiled because he was about to hit her with an offer she could not refuse. Refusal would result in her death.

"What the fuck you smiling for? This shit is far from funny asshole!" she said sarcastically.

"What if I told you that you can come work for me and make more money, have more power and more respect, than you can imagine?" He paused to let the statement sink in. "Under one circumstance. You cannot reveal that you work for me."

She looked around the room intrigued. "First of all, who the fuck are you? And second, what the fuck do you do?"

"My name is Special Agent Mike Heron. I work for the most powerful agency in the world: the Central Intelligence Agency, better known as the CIA."

She started laughing uncontrollably. "The CIA! You're kidding right? You work for the CIA and you want me to be a fucking spy?" She looked at his face to see if he was serious. "You are serious."

"As cancer." He gave her the coldest stare she'd ever seen. "Here's what's going to happen. You'll work directly under me. Your starting salary will be $150K a year plus perks. You'll be given more access to government operations than the FBI and all the police departments in the world combined. Basically, you'll be untouchable." He gave her his signature smug expression that men of power make when making life or death proposals.

"Let me get this straight." She looked around before looking

him in his eyes. *"The only reason you want me to work for you is because I'm a heroin addict who overdosed. All my friends died, and you're a good Samaritan who wants to save little old me."*

He touched her leg. *"Like I said, the $150K comes with perks for you. Let's just say this job comes with perks for me as well."* He slowly moved his hand up her thigh, close to her vagina.

When he got close to her vagina, she punched him in his mouth causing his lips to bleed. He responded with a swift smack to her face. The force of his smack sent her head crashing onto the bed. She looked up at him with an expression of passion that confused Agent Heron. She liked to be treated rough.

"Is that all you got?" She licked her lips. "This would be more fun if we were naked."

"I see." Agent Heron took a key from his pocket and uncuffed her. "Put your clothes on, we're out of here."

Sparrow was brought back to the present day from a beeping horn. She didn't realize how long she was in Lah-Lah Land reminiscing. "Oh shit!" she yelled. She was losing them.

She darted through traffic trying to find the white Rolls Royce Cullinan. The only problem with that was in Dubai, Rolls Royce was like a taxi. You see a thousand on the road.

"Fuck!" She saw three white Cullinan's' up ahead. She couldn't tell which one was them until she saw Dirty Redd with his head hanging out the window. "There goes my boy right there." She smiled at the thought that it was Dirty Redd that saved the day for her. "This is going to be fun."

She drove a safe distance behind them for the duration of the drive.

———

THE BULGARI RESORT
The lobby was covered with expensive marble and gold

fixtures throughout its massive space. If the lobby was an indication to what the room was going to look like, then it was paradise. The bellhop assisted them with the luggage to their suite. When they entered the plush dwelling, it was like they all took a deep sigh of disbelief of how decadent the suite was.

"I couldn't even imagine something like this, this—" Dirty Redd was at a loss of words.

"This shit is dope! Fuck all that fancy word shit. This the most fly suite I ever saw in my life," Prime said, finishing Dirty Redd's sentence.

They all glanced around the three-bedroom suite as if it were a little piece of heaven. It had a huge living room with a 100-inch flat screen tv mounted to the wall and sectional couches made from butter soft white leather. There was a huge kitchen and dining room fit for feeding ten people.

"Just show me the studio you were talking about," Mouf said to Mustafa. "I'm ready to go to work!"

"Yes, right this way." Mustafa escorted Mouf toward the studio area.

Dirty Redd watched as they strolled to the studio. "This guy is all work and no play," he said, referring to Mouf. "We just got here and all he wants to do is work."

"Facts! I'm trying to mingle with some of these Dubai baddies!" Prime responded in agreement with Dirty Redd.

"I saw a few downstairs at the bar by the lobby." Dirty Redd shook his head up and down as he looked at Prime, his partner in crime.

Prime looked at him, "Fuck it I'm down! Let's see what's good with these Dubai chicks."

They took the elevator back down to the lobby and strolled over to the bar/club. There were gorgeous women on the dance floor dancing with each other and kissing. There were a few at the bar, but they were accompanied by men. The venue was playing American rap music, which made Prime and Dirty Redd feel comfortable in this environment.

As they wandered through the club, they didn't notice the DJ looking in their direction. "We got the fucking Billigoats, Dirty Redd and Prime the God in the building!" With his last word, he played the groups biggest hit song to date: "Pockets."

The crowd went bonkers! Everyone began to sing along with the record. "You think that you the plug / well nigga I'm the socket / stop it / if getting money is the topic / you ain't getting no paper / if you ain't making profit / a prophet!"

The DJ played a whole set of the Billigoats greatest hits, which was limited because they only had one album. Nevertheless, that album had five hit songs on it. They were escorted to the VIP section and given two bottles of Ace of Spades on the house. The perks of being rap stars.

Sparrow was observing Dirty Redd, figuring out a way to get close to him. He was surrounded by the most beautiful women in Dubai. She had a plan to get close to him and say a few sweet nothings in his ear. First, she needed to lure him away from all the women.

She waited, then she saw the perfect opportunity. Dirty Redd was walking toward the bathroom. *Now is my chance,* she thought.

She walked in the same direction as Dirty Redd, timing her approach. When he was close enough, she made her move. She bumped into him so hard he thought she was a man.

"Excuse me, I'm so sorry. It's just that well I'm your biggest fan. I knew you wouldn't pay me any attention with all those beautiful women at your table." She put on her best *girl next door* act.

"You're okay," he said, catching eye contact with her. "You from the states?"

"Yes, I'm here for vacation. I couldn't believe my favorite rapper is here, too." She seductively stared in his eyes. She kept staring until she saw him stare back with the same sexual energy. "My name is Sarah, you need no introduction. Everyone in here knows the infamous Dirty Redd and the Billigoats."

"Nice to meet you, Sarah." He grabbed her hand and kissed it.

Shorty is kind of pretty in an innocent kind of way. It's something about her that I like, Dirty Redd thought.

"Can I ask you a question?" She stepped up the intensity of her tactics because it was working. "Do you believe in love at first sight?" she asked while seductively licking her lips.

"It depends on the situation." He was a sucker for love, but he didn't want to admit it. He couldn't break her stare.

I got him, she declared to herself. *Time to turn it up a notch.*

She grabbed his manhood. "I've been praying for this day, to be close to the man of my dreams." She felt his penis growing in her hands. "I'd give anything to spend just one night with Dirty Redd."

"We can make that happen," he said with his guard totally down.

"Come with me to my room." She grabbed his hand in hers and led the way as he followed.

That was easier than I thought. She opened the door to her lavish suite and passionately kissed him before leading him to her bedroom.

CHAPTER 3
MOUF & PRIME

Mouf was in the studio when Prime entered the suite with two sexy women in tow. They were passing the studio when Mouf noticed Dirty Redd was missing. "Yo Prime! Let me holla at you for a minute. Where the fuck is Dirty Redd?"

"He broke out with some broad," Prime responded.

"That's what I'm saying, you know you have to keep your eyes on him," Mouf said in an annoyed tone.

"Listen, that man is his own keeper. He is not in any harm, he met a chick and went to her suite. I'm sure he can handle himself." Prime shrugged his shoulders and shook his head to further prove his point.

Mouf made an expression that doubted Prime. "Whatever you say, but we both know Dirty Redd is a loose cannon. But you're right, he is his own man."

"I'm going to take these two to my room and I'll see you tomorrow bro'-ski." Prime started to escort the women to his room before stopping to ask a question of his own. "Where is Jay-Roc?"

"He has a suite on the other side. I heard his suite is better than this one." Mouf had an appearance of skepticism. "Can you believe that?"

"I'll have to see it to believe it," Prime replied with equal skepticism. "I'll see you in the a.m." When he moved the two beauties each grabbed an arm as if they were proud of this moment in time.

"Copy my dude," Mouf replied as he directed his attention back to the music he was creating.

Prime slowly strolled to his room. He knew they were going to be amazed when they saw how palatial it was. He opened the double doors to his room as if they were entering Utopia, and the two women mirrored his energy.

"Wow!" they both said in unison.

"This is breathtaking, we've never been inside any of these suites. We've only partied in the club downstairs," one of the women said with eyes wide.

"When you're royalty you spare no expense," Prime said with arrogance. "Now are you ladies ready?"

"Yeah!" they spoke in unison again, not knowing what they were getting ready for.

"We're going to play a little game called Simon Says." Prime shut the huge double doors.

———

THE IMPERIAL WING **OF THE BULGARI RESORTS**

The Imperial Wing of the Bulgari Resorts was exactly how it sounded: extravagant. There was real gold accenting Lux Touch Marble, the most expensive marble in the world, and a dinner table with ten chairs that resembled mini thrones. Then there was a twenty-foot window that spanned the whole length of the living room overlooking all of the skyscrapers of Dubai.

Mustafa escorted Jay-Roc, Tracy, and Lil' D-Boy around the spacious three-bedroom suite as if he was a designated tour guide. "Over here you have the world's first jacuzzi sauna." His eyes got wide before continuing, "You can soak and meditate while loosening up your limbs."

Jay-Roc looked at Mustafa strange for a second. *Mustafa is getting annoying. I need to get everyone settled so I can call D-Boy to let him know exactly where I'm at,* he thought to himself.

"And over here is a state-of-the-art home theater." Mustafa opened the doors to reveal an opulent room with a 100-inch screen. "Everything views in 5K 3D."

"Can you give us the grand tour tomorrow?" Jay-Roc asked, partly irritated. "We had a long day today and I need to make some important calls."

"I'll show the little prince to his room." He paused to point in another direction. "The master bedroom is down that hallway."

"Thank you for the hospitality." Jay-Roc shook his hand. "Good night, Mustafa."

"Good night, brother."

Mustafa began to escort Lil' D-Boy to his room. "This way little prince, I know you're going to love your room. I made sure it had every video game system available."

"Yes! I wanted to bring all of my game systems, but my dad said no," Lil' D-Boy said with excitement.

"You got it, buddy! Me and you are going to get along well, like best pals. Family." Mustafa looked at Lil' D-Boy and tears welled up in his eyes. "I have to go now, duty calls."

"Good night, Mr. Mustafa. Thanks for getting all the game systems installed in my room."

"Don't mention it." He wiped the tears that were falling. "It's the least I can do. Good night, buddy."

Mustafa made his way to the master suite. "One more stop." He started removing the layer of the mask that concealed his identity. As he was taking it off, a cell phone rang in his pocket. He looked at it and smiled. He let it keep ringing as he got closer to the master bedroom.

JAY-ROC WAS in the master bedroom waiting for D- Boy to answer the phone. "He never takes this long to answer my calls." He glanced at Tracy with a worried look. "I hope everything is good. This isn't like D-Boy."

"Don't jump to conclusions." She rubbed his shoulders. "He's probably resting or something," Tracy assured him.

Jay-Roc took a deep breath. "Yeah, you're right. I'm just anxious to see my brother—" he paused at the sound of a phone ringing outside of his door.

"Yo, do you hear that?" Jay-Roc asked sternly.

Tracy couldn't deny it. "Yes, who the fuck is that?" she responded with fear.

Jay-Roc quickly moved to his luggage where he concealed a Glock 9-mm. He grabbed it and cocked it back. "Get behind the dresser." She obliged while he moved closer to the door ready to empty the whole clip if need be.

Jay-Roc noticed that the phone was ringing in his hand and the phone on the other side of the door was ringing, too. He ended the call and the ringing stopped on the other side of the door. He called the number again and the ringing on the other side of the door began again, only this time someone answered.

"Hello." It was the voice of Mustafa.

"What the fuck is going on? Who is this? And how did you get this phone?" Jay-Roc demanded.

"This is Mustafa's phone, how did you get this number?" he laughed on the other side of the door.

Jay-Roc heard the voice speaking through the phone and from the other side of the door. "I don't know what type of game you playing but I'm about to open fire through this door in five seconds." He dropped the phone and tightly clutched his weapon with both hands. "Five, four, three, two—"

"Okay! Don't fucking shoot! It's me!"

27

"Me who?" Jay-Roc asked while keeping his finger on the trigger.

"It's your fucking brother, D-Boy!" D-Boy shouted.

Jay-Roc would notice that voice anywhere. He dropped his gun to the floor and opened the door to see D-Boy holding the mask that was Mustafa. "Get in here, you're a fucking asshole." He grabbed D-Boy in a bear hug and squeezed him like he did when they were kids.

D-Boy's back bones began to crack from the pressure of Jay-Roc's embrace. "Damn, Jay-Roc, you're cracking my back."

Jay-Roc let him go. "I can't believe this whole time you were posing as Mustafa." Jay-Roc looked at D-Boy with disbelief. "I had no idea, I mean the accent was on point with the mask and everything. You had me fooled."

"Me, too," Tracy said coming from behind the tall dresser. "It didn't even cross my mind." She approached D-Boy and hugged him. "It's good to see you, D-Boy."

"It's good to see you, too. I miss my family." Tears welled up in D-Boy's eyes, this time he let them fall.

They all hugged as a trio, a family. After the long embrace, Jay-Roc had a thousand questions. "So let me get this right. You and John both took acting classes and bought these professional Hollywood grade mask?"

"Yes, it was all John's idea." D-Boy looked him in the eye. "Remember John is an ex Israeli Intelligence Agent, so he knows all the tricks of the trade."

"Makes sense." Jay-Roc paused to formulate his next question. "So this is who you are all day every day when you step out?"

"No. We just started wearing these expensive disguises a week ago," D-Boy explained.

"Yo bro', I'm telling you man, you had me fooled beyond belief. I didn't even think at any time that you might have been Mustafa." Jay-Roc shook his head in disbelief. "Bro' you can come back to the states, and nobody would know you were Mustafa."

"One hundred percent," Tracy chimed in, "If you can fool your loved ones, the people that knew you the longest, you can fool anybody." She gave them both a matter-of-fact expression.

D-Boy looked at her before speaking, "That's exactly what me and John plan on doing."

"What do you mean, what you and John plan on doing?" Jay-Roc was confused.

"We're going to use your visit to Dubai to sneak back into the United States." D-Boy knew this was like an episode of Mission Impossible and he was Tom Cruise. "This year will make seven years since my death. The FEDS close cases after seven years so I should be good."

Jay-Roc was confused and happy at the same time. He looked around trying to soak it all in. It was a bit overwhelming to learn that your dead brother, who isn't dead, is returning from the dead.

"If anybody can pull it off, you and John can." Jay-Roc shook his head in agreement of his own statement. "After you guys pulled off your death and funeral without a glitch, I was convinced you could do the impossible."

"You have to keep this a secret. You can't even tell Lil' D-Boy." D-Boy scanned their faces to let them know the seriousness of his message. "He's too young to understand right now. When he gets a little older and he can handle it, I'll tell him myself."

"So that's the plan, you're coming back to America like Eddie Murphy," Jay-Roc said with glee in his tone.

"No, I'm coming back to America like D-Boy." D-Boy smiled at the thought of going home.

"The return of D-Boy."

CHAPTER 4
PALM JUMEIRAH, EMIRATES HILLS, DOWNTOWN DUBAI

Agents Bashir and Mohammed were getting restless and a bit angry. They have been staking out the condo high rise for a week with no sign of either American. What they didn't know was the men checked out under their old aliases and checked back in with new identities. An old intelligence buddy that owed John a favor gave him two state-of-the-art masks. These masks were designed to deceive the agents that were trained to detect masks. It was literally a new identity.

The two agents were parked in an all-black 2015 S-class 550 Mercedes Benz as an undercover vehicle. That is how wealthy Dubai is. Their Ubers are Rolls Royce, so their unmarked detective cars are Mercedes and BMW. The building they were facing was called The One, the most expensive apartment complex in the world. Apartments in this complex sold for as much as $74 million. The streets in front and on the side of the complex were lined with every luxury vehicle you could name. Perhaps the fact that Palm Jumeirah was an artificial island was the reason it was so expensive.

"What the fuck are these dudes doing in there?" Agent Bashir asked with sarcasm. "They must be fucking each other because neither one of them has come out for air."

Agent Mohammed concurred, "Exactly! Why would two grown men stay in a condo without coming out unless they're fucking each other?"

"You know the gay culture of Americans." Agent Bashir shook his head up and down as assurance to his next statement. "They love LGBTQ, and the other letters of their infidel organization."

They gave a hearty laugh at their constant anti-American rhetoric they loved to spew among each other. It made them feel validated when they both agreed on their anti-American sarcasm. The American agents did the same to the Arab agents. It was a hodgepodge of anti-ethnic hate among agents who claimed they wanted to save the world from terrorists.

As they were talking, they noticed an older Arab gentleman with a long red beard wearing expensive Arab garb exiting the building. He looked important from the way he glided as he walked with his head held noticeably high. He made a beeline directly to the two agents. They acknowledged him from the minute he exited the lavish condo complex.

"You see this guy coming directly toward us?" Agent Bashir asked his partner as if he wasn't seeing the same thing.

"Yeah, I see him." Agent Mohammed took out his service weapon and cocked it to make sure it was ready to fire. "If he makes one false move, I'm going to send him to Allah."

Agent Bashir took out his weapon and did the same. "I'm watching his every move, trust me. I'm trying to make it home to my wife's succulent lamb chops tonight."

The distinguished Arab man walked right up to the window and tapped on it hard three times. TAP! TAP! TAP!

Agent Bashir rolled down the window. "Can I help you, sir?" he said politely.

"Yes, you most certainly may assist me. Help is for disabled people," he replied arrogantly with a thick Arabic accent.

"Excuse me?" Agent Bashir replied with equal arrogance.

"You may be excused." He sashayed to the other side of the Mercedes and tapped again until the window was rolled down. "Now, let's see if we can try this again."

Agent Mohammed looked at his partner confused before turning back to address the gentleman. "How may I be of assistance to you?"

"That's better." He closed his eyes and shook his head up and down. "My name is Rahman and I'm a longtime resident of this complex. I've noticed you guys' parking at various locations around this building." Rahman paused and got closer to Agent Mohammed's face before continuing, "Is there someone in this building under investigation or something?"

The two agents looked at each other before Agent Mohammed spoke. "What would make you think we're detectives?"

"Well for one, the department issued weapons you both have on your laps says your cops or robbers." Rahman smiled at his own cynicism. "Also the fact that your car is a 2015. No one around here drives a Mercedes that old with tints that dark but a Dubai undercover police officer."

"What would make you come to that conclusion?" this Time Agent Bashir spoke. "Maybe we can't afford the new one. Doesn't mean we're police officers."

"Oh, but on the contrary." Rahman pointed to a balcony with a green light coming from it. "Do you see that green light coming from the balcony on the twenty-fifth floor?"

The two agents strained their necks to see it from inside the car, but they were able to see it. "What about it?" Agent Mohammed asked.

The green light was a diversion, and while they struggled to see it, Rahman swiftly placed a tracking device by the doors' handle. When they were finished trying to see the light, they turned their attention back to Rahman. He had a self-assured expression on his face because the detectives didn't see his sleight of hand.

"That's my condo. From up there I can see everything on the ground. So, while you guys have been watching the complex, I've been watching you." Rahman gave them a creepy look to add emphasis to his revelation.

"Enough with the fucking games, old man!" Agent Bashir was losing his patience. "What do you want? And no more fucking riddles!"

"It's simple what I want." He stopped to crack his neck before speaking. "I want you and your goofy partner to get the fuck out of here and go somewhere else with your bullshit." His smile turned serious.

Agent Mohammed got out of the Mercedes. "Who the fuck do you think you are talking to like that?" He squared up face to face as if he was going to punch Rahman in the jaw.

"I am Rahman Ibn Abdullah, one of the first settlers of Dubai, emissary to Sheikh Mohammed bin Rashid Al Maktoum." Rahman prompted his nose higher in the air with his last statement.

"I wouldn't give a fuck if you were his brother." Agent Mohammed snarled. "If you interfere with an official Dubai criminal investigation, we will lock your ass up and you will not get out. Not before we humiliate you."

"I see." Rahman rubbed on his long red beard. "Me and you both know that would be a huge mistake. One you cannot afford." Rahman looked them square in their eyes. "Have a great evening, and may Allah bless you." He strolled back into the expensive apartment complex as if he were floating on air.

Agent Bashir looked at his partner confused and angered. "The nerve of that asshole!"

They both got back into the Mercedes and neither one spoke until the dispatch announced, "Calling all cars to a robbery in progress! The Hills near Downtown Dubai, there are two armed gunmen taking jewelry from a Tiffany Jewelry store on West Fourth and Palm Street."

"We might as well get some action," Agent Bashir started up the car.

"Anything beats this crap," Agent Mohammed agreed as the vehicle leaped into gear speeding toward the robbery.

THE TWENTY-FIFTH FLOOR OF THE ONE LUXURY APARTMENT COMPLEX

Apartment number 2503 was the door Rahman opened. He quickly turned the green light off and made his way to the balcony where a high-powered telescope sat on a tripod facing the two agents. This telescope was equipped with a high-powered mic that could detect the vibration of the human voice from a distance up to 1,500 feet, so Rahman was able to hear them as well. He watched them as they sped off.

Rahman laughed at the recording of the two Arab agents making fun of American agents. He also found it hilarious that they didn't know that he swiftly placed a tracking device by the car's passenger door handle when he went from one side to the other. They were oblivious to Rahman watching and listening to them for three days while they were staking out the complex.

He played back the recording of the two Dubaian agents. *"They must be fucking each other because neither one of them has come out for air."*

"Exactly! Why would two grown men stay in a condo without coming out unless they're fucking each other?"

"You know the gay culture of Americans. They love LGBTQ, and the other letters of their infidel organization."

Rahman stopped the recording. "We will see who is going to get fucked." Rahman laughed at his thoughts before picking up his cellphone. It rang twice before it was answered, as planned.

If this line were to ring three times, it means the line is compromised.

"I was right about our little friends. I just had an interesting altercation with them, but I was able to plant a tracker on the vehicle. Let us see what turns up," Rahman spoke in a measured tone.

"I see, so what is our next move since we know we may have been compromised?"

"To proceed with Project Exodus as planned." Rahman paused. "I don't think we have much to worry about from these two rookies. I just came up with an alternate plan for them."

"Copy. I'll see you later as planned." The line went dead.

Rahman looked out into the horizon as he spoke to himself, "This is going to be so much fun." He remarked at the plans he had for Agents Bashir and Muhammad, "They're never going to see it coming."

BULGARI RESORTS

Dirty Redd closed his eyes in pure ecstasy while Sparrow went down on him under the covers to perform fellatio on him. Like clockwork, she made sure he got his morning session before his eyes were open. Then a conversation and breakfast followed by the second session. More conversation followed by lunch and then the third session. The last two sessions would be dinner, then a late-night session before falling asleep, only to be repeated the next day. This had gone on for three days now.

She was skilled in the art of seduction, and her methods were simple yet complex. She was draining Dirty Redd of all the semen in his body to render him weak and emotionally attached. Her conversations were psychologically controlling his mental and spiritual energy to the point where he would ultimately surrender all his power to her.

Dirty Redd's phone was ringing. "Babe I have to answer the phone." He struggled to reach for his phone. That's when

35

Sparrow abruptly leaped from under the cover and grabbed Dirty Redd's phone.

"Nope! You're all mine," she said, pretending to be playing. "I'm not letting you go until I say I'm ready." She let out a girlish giggle for the effect.

"No seriously!" He forcefully grabbed his phone from her hand. "I have to talk to my team. They haven't seen me in three days. They are probably worried and mad because I always do shit like this." He answered the phone.

"Where the fuck are you?" Mouf shouted into the phone. "You haven't laid down any of your verses for any of the songs we wrote. You are so far up this bitch's ass, that if she farts it'll blow your fucking brains out!"

Dirty Redd laughed knowing he shouldn't have done it out loud. "That shit was funny. It sounds like a bar, fart and blow your brains out."

"I'm glad you find this shit funny, because I'm two seconds from quitting this group and going solo, my dude!" Mouf said with sincerity before hanging up.

The vibe just turned serious. Everyone knew Mouf was the backbone of the group. Without Mouf there was no group, and they all knew it. Mouf was a triple threat; he wrote, produced, and performed very well. He was the one that formed the group. Dirty Redd came up with the name for his clothing line, but Mouf is the one who came up with the thought that they should call the group the Billigoats.

Dirty Redd got up from the bed, only to be pulled back by Sparrow. "I told you... you can't leave until I say so." She swiftly threw him on his back and straddled herself tightly onto his groin.

Dirty Redd struggled to free himself from her hold, but her leg muscles were too strong. She could kill him within ten seconds with her hands from the training she received from the

AMERICAN D-BOY II

CIA. Dirty Redd felt the pressure of her hold and he really tried harder to free himself to no avail.

Dirty Redd began to panic. "Yo! Get the fuck off me!" He wiggled his body as she gave him a sadistic look. "Bitch if you don't get the fuck off me!"

"The only way I'll get off you is if you take me with you." She paused to see his reaction. "I promise I won't get in the way."

"Okay! Just get off me." He quickly got up and put his clothes on.

She was already getting dressed and at the door waiting for Dirty Redd. "After you, my dear."

"How the fuck did you get dressed that fast?" Dirty Redd asked curiously.

Sparrow smiled. "I'm a woman on the go, so I speed dress all the time."

"Whatever you say."

She opened the door and they both exited her suite, headed for his.

That was a close call, he was about to break the hold I was putting on his mind. Time to implement phase two, Sparrow thought. *This is going to be the fun part.*

"Dirty Redd," Sparrow said in the sweetest voice she could muster.

"Yes baby?" he replied with equal reverence.

"I think I love you." She looked him in his eyes for effect.

Dirty Redd stopped in his tracks and returned the stare she was giving him before speaking. "I love you, too, Sarah."

I got him!

They continued to stroll to his apartment hand in hand.

CHAPTER 5
THE ROYAL WING OF THE BULGARI RESORT

D-Boy was in full Mustafa mode when he entered Lil' D-Boy's room. "Grand rising, young prince!" he said in a jovial tone. "I have lots of fun things to do today, just me and you."

Lil' D-Boy was just waking up, so he was rubbing his eyes and stretching. He was feeling the effects of jetlag on his developing body. "Good morning, Mustafa. What were you saying again? Me and you are going to do what?"

"Pardon me, allow me to give you a minute to get your bearings before I bombard you with this good news." He paused and took a deep breath before speaking. "I was informing you of the wonderful events I have scheduled for you and I today."

"Just you and I? What about Mom and Dad?" He looked confused.

"They want to spend some alone time together, you know get romantic." He saw that his explanation wasn't working, so he sat on the bed. "Me and your father are like brothers, although he never mentioned me. We are closer than people understand, but that is between me and you. No one else but me, you, and your parents need to know about this."

Lil' D-Boy stood up. "Where is my dad?" He moved toward the door.

Right before he reached for the doorknob, his father opened the door. He noticed his son's distressed demeanor. "What's wrong, Lil' D?"

"Mustafa was telling me I was going with him, and you and Mom weren't coming so I wanted to hear it from you. I mean, I don't really know Mustafa like that." He paused. "Besides, you always told me to never talk to or go anywhere with a stranger."

Jay-Roc hugged his son tight. "It's okay, Lil' D. You're right, never talk to a stranger, but Mustafa is like my brother. We're just as close as me and my real brother, D-Boy, the man you were named after."

"So, what you're saying is that Mustafa isn't a total stranger, and he's close to you like Uncle D-Boy that is in heaven." The innocence of his confusion showed on his face.

"Exactly! Mustafa is close to me like my brother. You can trust him with your life."

Jay-Roc saw the tension release from his son's little body as his mind put what he'd been told in perspective. "I get it now." Lil' D-Boy turned around and walked up to Mustafa. "I'm sorry about running away from you. Now that I know you are close to my dad, we can be best friends."

D-Boy grabbed Lil' D-Boy and hugged him, holding him for an extended period. "I'm going to be the best friend you ever had." He freed him from the loving embrace and looked Lil' D-Boy in his eyes. "Whenever you need anything, I mean anything in the world, you just call me, and I will make sure your wish is my command." He stepped back and displayed a kowtow.

Lil' D-Boy giggled. "You funny, Mustafa."

Mustafa grabbed his hand. "This way, young prince. I must show you all the wonders of Dubai." He stopped to greet Jay-Roc. "I'll meet you back here at one o'clock sharp."

"Copy." Jay-Roc kneeled down so he could be eye to eye with Lil' D-Boy. "You listen to Mustafa and be careful like I taught you."

"Yes, Daddy, I'll watch my surroundings and I won't talk to strangers." He was able to regurgitate his father's lessons on command.

"That's right!" Jay-Roc hugged him. "I love you, buddy."

"I love you, too, Daddy."

"I'll see you here at one p.m.," Mustafa repeated.

"I got you, one o'clock sharp."

As they walked out of the door Jay-Roc got a call from Prime. "What's going on, Bossman?" Prime was the only member to call Jay-Roc by that moniker.

"What's going on, Prime?" Jay-Roc detected something was wrong from Prime's tone.

"You need to come over to the suite and talk to Mouf." Prime put the speaker phone on so Jay-Roc could hear Mouf in the background ranting.

"Let me guess, it has something to do with Dirty Redd."

"Don't it always? But this time Mouf is talking about leaving the group."

"I'll be right there." Jay-Roc hung up the phone and rushed through the door on his way to the Billigoat suite.

——————

BILLIGOAT SUITE

When Dirty Redd and Sparrow reached the door to the suite, they could hear Mouf fuming. Dirty Redd took the keycard from his pocket and paused before unlocking the door. He took a deep breath and paused a bit longer. The anxiety was building up in him so much he began to shake slightly. He contracted severe PTSD from being incarcerated, so his nervousness was visible.

"Are you okay?" Sparrow asked while rubbing his shoulder.

"Not really." He took another deep breath. "I have anxiety from PTSD… it's a long story."

"We have time, but for now you have to get yourself together and go in there like a general, a warrior. Defeat all your enemies. You are Dirty Redd the Conqueror." Sparrow was using an old trick that the CIA taught her.

"Take advantage of every crisis. If there isn't one, create it. Sow seeds of dissension to divide the nucleus of any group. Then they are ripe for the conquering," said Agent Heron.

Sparrow was quick witted and recalled that lesson as if it were a computer file ready to use on impulse. She saw her efforts take effect in his mind because he was shaking his head in agreement to her every word. His facial expression went from stressful to defiant in a split second.

"You're right, I'm Dirty Redd the Conqueror!" his anxiety turned into aggression.

"You don't need them, all you need is me, baby." She grabbed his face and passionately kissed him. "You got this, baby."

Dirty Redd opened the door and both Prime and Mouf diverted their attention to first Dirty Redd then Sarah. They all stood there without saying a word. Mouf was staring at Dirty Redd and Sarah with venom. Dirty Redd stared back with equal energy.

"You got something you want to say to me?" Dirty Redd broke the silence.

"Word! That's what you have to say to me my nigga? After all the blood sweat and tears I put into this group, that's what you have to say to me?" Mouf was shaking from anger as he spoke.

"What you want me to say? I'm sorry. Well, I'm not! You're mad because I came to Dubai and decided to hang out a little before getting to work. That's on you," Dirty Redd said defiantly.

Mouf stepped to Dirty Redd face to face. "Don't try to front like this is new because you got her here. This shit has been going on for the longest and you know it. You got one more time to pull one of your stunts and I'm going solo."

"You always say that shit like we supposed to be scared because big bad Mouf is leaving the group. Boo hoo. I don't give a fuck if you leave, I'm tired of rap anyway!" Dirty Redd was inches from Mouf's face.

Mouf pushed Dirty Redd and he flew back six feet. "Get the fuck out of my face! You meet this bitch and now you want to get it popping! Let's get it then!" Mouf put his hands up in a fighting position.

"Yeah, that's what I'm talking about." Dirty Redd put his hands up as well and moved toward Mouf.

As they were squaring up to fist fight, Jay-Roc entered the suite and quickly stood in front of the two men. "What the hell is going on? I leave you guys alone for a couple of days and this is what you do! That's what's wrong with Black people, you make it out of the ghetto, but you can't take that ghetto shit out of you! I told you guys to leave that street shit back home. Do not bring that shit to Dubai or anywhere for that matter, because street shit gets in the way of the bag every time. You understand?"

There was a short pause before Mouf spoke, "I understand but the problem is I don't think Dirty understands that. We all know Dirty be fucking up, but we just stand by and watch him do it."

"He has a point, Dirty. You're always late, hell sometimes you don't even show up," Jay-Roc said in corroboration with Mouf.

Mouf took Jay-Roc's declaration as vindication before speaking. "You never know which person you're going to get. Dirty is messy and late, Redd shows up and gets the job done." Mouf hesitated before continuing. "All I'm saying is in order for me to stay in this group, I need Redd to show up more than Dirty."

Dirty Redd stood there with Sarah standing next to him but slightly behind him, holding onto his left arm. She made sure to always keep human contact with him to further seduce him. She knew he was on her hook already, now it was a matter of using him to complete her mission. She was also giving him confidence to go against the grain of the group.

"I hear what you're saying, but there is a method to my madness that I didn't hear any of you say." He paused and looked at Mouf and Jay-Roc. Prime was out of the conversation because he was neutral. "Did you consider that when I'm not rapping in the booth, I'm designing fashion? I am in the top ten of urban fashion as we speak. Honestly, the only reason I rap is because my heart is in the music, but my passion is fashion."

"That sounds good for you, but my passion is this music. You are fucking up this bag trying to be a fashion designer and a rapper," Mouf said calmly but sternly.

"He has a point, Dirty. The clothing line is dope and I stand behind it," Jay-Roc paused. "You have to find a way to balance them both, so you won't interfere with the music bag, and we're not slowing up your fashion bag."

Dirty Redd laughed. "I hear you all talking about bags, let me tell you something. I made more in six months from the Billigoat clothing line than the Billigoat rap group ever made me! Honestly, I can stop rapping today and I'll be good for life." Dirty Redd had a smug expression on his face.

Sparrow squeezed Dirty Redd's arm to let him know she was with him. She made sure to stay inconspicuous but present. She didn't want to seem like she was the motivation behind Dirty Redd's newfound aggression toward the group, although she was. Every move he was making was a direct result of Sparrow's planning. On the outside she held an expression of innocence and naivety, but inside she had a sinister scowl.

"So, what are you saying, my nigga?" Mouf asked in a fed-up tone. "Everyone knows the Billigoat clothing line is popping. You want to know why?" Mouf hesitated. "Because of the success of the Billigoat rap group, that's why. Before I told you we should call the group after your clothing line, it wasn't selling shit. I remember you coming to me crying about your sales, that's when I came up with the idea to start a group named after your clothing line. Now you are throwing it in our face about how much money you made in six months. That's because we made your shit hot, not you."

Dirty Redd was silent. Sparrow started pinching his arm trying to get him to say something slick as a rebuttal. There was nothing he could say. Mouf was right. The Billigoat clothing line didn't take off until the Billigoat group was formed. The clothing line took on a life of its own, but it was after the success of the group.

"You right, my G, the clothing line did blow up after the group. It still doesn't take away from the fact that I put in the work to blow up the clothing line. I didn't see one of you lift a finger to help me with the designs. But I see you with your hand out every time I get a big check," Dirty Redd spoke with defiance. Sparrow squeezed his shoulder instead of pinching his arm as a sign of approval.

Prime noticed how close Sparrow was to Dirty Redd. As he gazed closer at her face, he could not help but think to himself, *she looks so familiar. I can't put my finger on it, but I've seen her before.*

Sparrow spotted Prime observing her suspiciously. *Fuck! I think my cover is blown!*

Sparrow turned her head away from his view so he couldn't see her face clearly. That made her seem more suspicious to Prime. The tension in the air was thick. Mouf and Dirty Redd still didn't resolve their dispute. To add to that, Prime was onto Sparrow, and she knew it. It was only a matter of time before he made the connection.

"Alright, let's focus on what's important," Jay-Roc announced. "I have the perfect solution to this problem. Mouf is right, he does put in a lot of work with the group. And Dirty is right, he puts in a lot of work for his clothing line. I have a deal on the table for $700K a piece for all three of you to go solo on American D-Boy Records."

There was a strange silence in the room after Jay-Roc spoke. It changed the energy in everyone's mind. It also detoured Prime's attention away from Sparrow, and onto the prospect of that $700K signing bonus to go solo. Jay-Roc had been toying with the idea before coming to Dubai. Now was the perfect time to spring his new plan on the team.

"I was thinking about this move for some time." Jay-Roc paused for the effect. "Now I see the resolution to this problem is to give you guys solo deals. And after you rock your solo projects, you can come back together, and I'll give you another $700K a piece to do a third Billigoat album. How does that sound?" Jay-Roc knew it was an offer they could not refuse considering they only got $250K a piece for the first two Billigoat albums.

"That sounds dope, Jay-Roc," Mouf was the first to chime in. "I'm all for it, sounds like a great plan to me." Mouf glanced at Dirty Redd and Prime. "What you think?"

"When was a cool million to rap ever a problem?" Prime said sarcastically.

Dirty Redd was the only one that didn't agree. "What about you, Dirty?" Jay-Roc asked, noticing Dirty Redd was the only one not excited about the new deal.

"If I go solo, I'm going independent. I have enough money to start my own record label," Dirty Redd said arrogantly. "I already got the name and the LLC for my label. It's called Billigoat Music Group."

This was a complete shock to everyone. Dirty Redd was concealing this news for the right moment which was now. It caught them all off guard, but the person most astonished was Jay-Roc. He looked at Dirty Redd as an asset to his label because of the success of the Billigoat clothing line. Losing him as an artist would have an impact on his bottom line.

"When were you going to tell us?" Jay-Roc asked.

"I actually was going to announce it after this tour," Dirty Redd responded.

"Wow, this is definitely going to change the plan," Jay-Roc said with uncertainty.

"So technically this was going to be my last album with the group. I'll get back to you about doing the third Billigoat album when we finish the tour." When Dirty Redd said that last statement, he exited the suite with Sparrow in tow.

When Dirty Redd and Sparrow left the suite, everyone was silent. Each person was left with their own opinions of the whole situation. For Mouf, he was content with the new deal Jay-Roc put on the table. It gave him exactly what he wanted, a solo deal and more money. He had a plan to start his own clothing line with any extra future money, and this deal was it.

Prime had different thoughts racing through his mind. He wanted to invest in real estate with any money he got from the music industry. There was something else that kept picking at his thoughts. It was Sparrow. He couldn't help but think about her presence in the room. He wanted to get to the bottom of what his intuition was telling him.

I don't know what it is, but something is telling me that she might be trying to do more than lock my boy down. If it's something else, it'll reveal itself. I'll just keep my eyes on her.

CHAPTER 6
SPARROW'S SUITE

Dirty Redd was sitting on the bed, talking on the phone to Rob, his partner with the Billigoat clothing line. Rob was the Creative Director of Billigoat brand clothing. He ran day-to-day operations and did most of the designs. They were from two different worlds. Rob was a clean-cut Irish man in his fifties who played bass guitar in a rock band, and Dirty Redd was a former drug dealer who rapped. Despite their differences, they shared a mutual love for fashion design.

Oddly enough, Rob created most of the popular urban designs that made Billigoat a household name. They both decided to keep that a secret and tell the world Dirty Redd was the chief designer to enhance the allure of the brand. In short, Rob was a Billigoat, because without Rob dedicating his energy to creating great designs there would be no Billigoat fashion.

Dirty Redd knew this, so he made sure he took care of Rob first when the money came in. They developed a great system that worked for the company. Dirty Redd stayed relevant in the music industry and that kept the Billigoat clothing line relevant and brought in the money. The minute the Billigoat rap group failed, the clothing line would fall as well.

"You have to stay in the Billigoat group, or this clothing line will sink!" Rob said in his signature monotone. "I don't get you sometimes, Dirty. How can you not see the groups success is the clothing line's success?"

"You're right, but I can't keep letting Mouf think I need him," Dirty Redd spoke in the same monotone whenever he spoke to Rob. It was a habit he developed from being around Rob so much. "He keeps reminding me it was his idea to name my clothing line after the rap group and that's the only reason the Billigoat clothing line is popping. Although he's right, I don't need that thrown in my face every time we have a disagreement."

"I think we're way past that point. It's not a question of *if you need the group,* the question is *does the group need you?* If they decide to ditch you because of your behavior and disband altogether, then I'm afraid this clothing line is going to fall faster than it rises."

Sparrow sat behind Dirty Redd while he spoke on the phone with Rob as she thought about her next move. She came up with a thought and almost activated it but decided to delay it.

He's going to eat it up if I tell him I think I may be pregnant. It's too early. We just met four days ago. I'll give it another week before I spring that one on him.

While she was in her thoughts, Dirty Redd hung up the phone and turned around to face her before speaking. "I think I fucked up. I should have been more understanding about why Mouf was so upset. There's more to it than you know. I've been fucking up, getting by on talent. Other people do the work and I take the credit. Like the clothing line, yeah, I came up with the logo, but Rob does most of the dope designs."

"That doesn't mean you have to take his verbal abuse. So what Rob does most of the work? Tesla invented everything and Edison took credit. It's one of the forty-eight laws of power." Sparrow poured fuel on a fire that Dirty Redd was trying to put out.

"What do you mean that's one of the forty-eight laws of power?" Dirty Redd asked with a confused expression.

What an idiot, Sparrow thought before speaking. *"The 48 Laws of Power* is a book written by Robert Greene detailing the history of how the most powerful people came to that power. He refers to the tactics they use as laws. You are just using your natural born talent to be a powerful leader." She kissed him passionately for effect then looked him in his eyes to see his reaction.

Just like a lost little puppy in my hands.

She began to stroke his bald head as if she were petting a dog. "Don't worry baby, your clothing line will be okay with or without them."

"You think so, babe?" he stared into her eyes.

"I know so. You don't have to bow to anyone. You're the king."

She saw his eyes light up. "You right, I'm the king! You can't talk to me like I'm a peasant!" Dirty Redd roared.

"That's right, baby!"

She kept stroking and smiling at him while thinking, *this is going to be the best mission I've ever been on.*

———

JAY-ROC'S SUITE

D-Boy and Lil' Dee were coming in from a whole day of playing, running, soaring, swinging, and riding on every ride at the IMG Worlds of Adventure theme park. Lil' Dee was worn out from the day of activities. So was D-Boy, who had to keep up his facade as Mustafa for the whole six hours. The longest that he had to endure being Mustafa was an hour. That was when Jay-Roc and the Billigoats landed in Dubai.

This whole pretending to be a Middle Eastern tour guide is wearing me the fuck out, D-Boy protested to himself.

As they entered the palatial suite they were greeted by Jay-Roc and Tracy. Lil' Dee ran toward them as fast as he could. "Mommy! Daddy! I had the best time ever with Uncle Mustafa. We went on every ride! We went on the Hulk ride, and the Avengers ride! We even did the longest roller coaster ride in the world!" Lil' Dee ranted with excitement.

Jay-Roc picked Lil' Dee up in his arms. "I'm glad you got to bond with your Uncle Mustafa. See I told you he was a cool dude."

He smiled at his father. "Yeah, he is the best uncle in the world!" Lil' Dee replied.

"Come on, Lil' Dee, let's get you ready for bed," Tracy said as she took Lil' Dee's hand and led him to the huge bathroom area to take a bath.

That left Jay-Roc and D-Boy alone to discuss their plans on getting D-Boy back into the states. John had to be in on this plan as well. He was the orchestrator of the plan to fake their deaths. John was a mastermind, a tactician when it came to a well thought out strategy.

"Where's John?" Jay-Roc asked.

"He should be here any minute now," D-Boy replied.

Jay-Roc gave D-Boy a worried look before speaking. "I hope he isn't being followed."

"John is a professional spy. I doubt anyone is following him without him knowing."

Just as D-Boy finished his last sentence his cell phone rang. "Speaking of the devil. This is John calling me now." D-Boy answered the phone. "Hey Johnny Boy, you here?"

John rang the doorbell. "I'm here."

Jay-Roc opened the door, and when he saw who was there, he almost shut the door in the man's face. He didn't recognize him at all. "John?"

"My name is Rahman Mohammed," the man replied in a thick Arab accent.

Jay-Roc looked confused. "Rahman? Where the fuck is John?"

John winked his eye. "It's me," he whispered.

Jay-Roc opened the door wide and let John enter the luxury suite. "My main man Johnathon Gillespie! You are still the master of disguise. This is the second time you fooled me. The first time you were a bum, this disguise is a step up."

"I would agree, because this character is royal as opposed to the bum I played." John smiled as he went to shake Jay-Roc's hand.

"Bring it in!" Jay-Roc grabbed John and squeezed him with all his might.

"I can't breathe," John protested.

"My bad. I didn't recognize my own strength."

"What's good, Johnny Boy? Did you shake those two dimwitted detectives?"

"For the time being, but I have something planned for those two before we leave Dubai." John smiled at D-Boy.

"Knowing you, whatever you have planned is going to be a blast to say the least." D-Boy smiled back at him.

"First things first, let's get the specifics of our return to America." John made sure he had both men's attention before continuing. "This has to be as stealth as possible. Because we are traveling with an entourage it gives us cover. I will pose as the the road manager for the Arab leg of the tour. When the Arab part of the tour is over, Jay-Roc will keep me on for the state side of the tour."

"What about me? What part I'm I going to play on the tour?" D-Boy asked.

"You can stay on as a babysitter to Lil' D-Boy, and as an adviser for the Billigoats while in the Arab Emirates. Again, when the tour is ready to go to America you'll ask to come to America with the crew. Of course, Jay-Roc is going to say yes." John looked into both men's eyes to see if they understood.

"That sounds like a plan to me," Jay-Roc said in compliance with John.

"Another thing, me and D-Boy don't know each other. We just met today. We don't need any of the guys to make any connections."

"Got it," D-Boy chimed in. "One more thing, we have to be able to take the disguise off at least once a week to take a real shower. I know it's going to be difficult to do on the bus with the Billigoats there, but I'm not trying to look and smell like a musky Arab."

"You're kidding me, right?" John replied, "I don't know about you, but every time we stop I'm going to a hotel to shower and relax without the disguise for a few hours while the Billigoats perform."

"So that's what I'm doing, too! I'm not trying to be a funky ass Arab. It's bad enough my disguise got me looking like a weirdo," D-Boy said.

"It's better to look like a weirdo than to be dead or locked up for the rest of your life," Jay-Roc commented.

"Facts!" D-Boy concurred.

"We have three shows in Dubai. The first one is at the Dubai Media Amphitheater, the second one is at The Fridge and last we're at The Music Hall. Then we go to Abu Dhabi for three shows. Our last stop is the Arab Emirates at Al Sharjah for two shows," Jay-Roc informed.

"Give me a complete list of the tour dates so I can do some logistic preparation," John instructed Jay-Roc.

"Will do. Anything else you need to know?" Jay-Roc asked.

"I need the full name and date of birth of everyone who will be on the tour bus with us so I can do a thorough background check. You can never be too safe," John said with a serious expression, "You'll never know until you look."

"Facts!" That was D-Boy's favorite phrase.

"Okay gentlemen, I have some business to attend to with the

Billigoats. I'll see you back here in a couple hours. Maybe we can have dinner together, on me?" Jay-Roc proposed.

"Hell yeah! It's about time you bought something for me," D-Boy said jokingly.

"I got you, little brother." Jay-Roc walked toward the door. "See you in a few." He exited, headed for the Billigoat suite.

When Jay-Roc left the suite John looked at D-Boy with concern. "What's the matter John?"

"I was just thinking about Murphy's Law."

"What's Murphy's Law?" D-Boy asked as if he was in class.

"Anything that can go wrong, will go wrong," John replied.

"That don't sound like a law. It sounds more like speaking disaster into existence."

"Trust me, it's not. It's just expecting the best but preparing for the worst."

BILLIGOAT SUITE

As Jay-Roc approached the door to the Billigoat suite, he was greeted by Dirty Redd and his new girlfriend, Sarah. Dirty Redd held his head down because he knew Jay-Roc was perturbed about him leaving the label. The two men never had a disagreement, so this was a very awkward moment. They both stood at the door silently, waiting for the other to break the ice.

"So, are you really leaving the label to start your own?" Jay-Roc asked with humility.

"I don't know what I'm doing. I'm just tired of Mouf telling me if it wasn't for him naming my clothing line after the group it wouldn't be shit," Dirty Redd replied.

"I mean, he's right about his idea to name the line Billigoats. But I do get where you're coming from. The Billigoat clothing line is your creation, and we are all very proud of your accomplishments," Jay-Roc paused.

"But—" Dirty Redd filled in the blank pause.

"But you're both right, in my opinion. All of us work together like a machine, with each man representing a part in the success of everything. Don't be egotistical. We know you're the man with the clothing, and you must give Mouf his props for his incredible rap skills that helped propel the group to the top. He works very hard for the group. All he really wants is for you to be more responsible."

Sparrow stood quietly as the two men spoke. She started to nudge him but didn't want it to seem obvious that she was influencing his decisions. She knew Jay-Roc would sense something because he wasn't under her spell. She had to play it safe while around the team. It would be easy for them to detect her devious ideas. So, she projected herself as an innocent woman with no ulterior motives.

I came too far to fumble the ball now, she thought.

Jay-Roc looked at her. "I'm sorry for being so rude. I'm Jay-Roc, the CEO and owner of American D-Boy Records. And you are?" He stuck his hand out for a formal handshake.

Sparrow firmly shook his hand. "Hi, I'm Sarah. I'm such a fan of your label. I go back seven years when you had Shoota on the label."

"Okay, you're an official fan of the label. Since you're with Dirty, you're an honorary member of the Billigoats."

"Oh, thank you so much, Jay-Roc." She pretended to blush and to really care about his offer. "I will represent to the fullest."

"Great! Now let's go in here and fix this mess." Jay-Roc looked at Dirty Redd. "Can you let bygones be bygones and talk it over in a civilized manner with your brother, Mouf?"

"Yeah, I guess so." Dirty Redd used his key card to open the door.

When they entered the suite, Mouf and Prime were sitting on a white leather sofa waiting for Jay-Roc to arrive. When Mouf and Prime saw Dirty Redd and Sparrow, they both changed their vibration. Their last conversation with Dirty Redd was him telling them he was starting his own label.

Prime paid close attention to Sparrow, and she noticed it. She tried to stay out of his focus for fear that he would make the connection with her and the magazine reporter back in New York. Prime wouldn't stop looking at her, his senses were tingling. He had that feeling he had seen her before.

I can't put my finger on where I saw this chick before. Something about her eyes, I've seen them somewhere recently, Prime thought.

He noticed her trying to conceal her face from him because he was staring. *He's on to me,* Sparrow thought.

She could tell he saw her trying to hide from him, so she just played it cool and stopped the charade. She let him stare and just tried to blend in by holding on to Dirty Redd's arm. It was something she kept doing to let him know she was in control and remind him that she was right by his side always.

Prime would have known her immediately if it were not for the red wig, and the huge horn-rimmed glasses she wore at the press conference in New York. Now she wore a jet-black wig with angel blue eyes making her appear as if she wouldn't harm an ant when she could probably kill every man in the room with her bare hands. Make no mistake, Sparrow was a highly skilled killer, trained by the best: the masters at the CIA headquarters in Langley, Virginia.

"What's good, Mouf?" Dirty Redd said breaking the silence. "I want to apologize for the way I've been handling myself in this group. You're right to get upset about my behavior. I want to do better."

Mouf stood up with a serious expression, then he smiled and gave Dirty Redd a brotherly hug. "That's all I wanted to hear, my G, that you give a fuck because it was feeling like it was all about you. We're a team, and there's no I in team."

Prime stood up and joined the gathering. "Word Dirt, that's

all we both wanted. You're a real man for at least admitting where you were wrong." Prime shook Dirty Redd's hand and hugged him. "I love you, my nigga. We go back before any of this music shit!"

"That's real, my G," Dirty Redd replied. "We go back to like first grade. I knew you before I knew Mouf before I knew anyone in this room."

"I don't mean to interrupt this bromance," Jay-Roc said jokingly. "Does this mean the group is staying together, we can do the solo projects I mentioned and get to this super-bag of money?"

"That's what the fuck I'm talking about!" Prime said with vigor.

"Fuck yeah!" Mouf said. "We in Dubai, my nigga! Let's live it up and celebrate!"

"That's what I was saying from the get-go!" Dirty Redd agreed.

Sparrow stood on the outside of the masculine circle of men. She had mixed feelings. One side was adoring the fraternal display. It was uplifting and encouraging. While on the other side she had a job to do, and this was counterproductive to her mission. There was nothing she could do but go along with the energy of the moment.

As she stood smiling, she noticed Prime staring directly in her face again. This time she made eye contact with him instead of looking away. She smiled and tried another approach. She tried to entice him by licking her lips. He couldn't help himself from getting a rise from her efforts. She saw it was working when he didn't shy away from her. This time she winked her eye. He looked away and joined back in the group's affairs.

I may have been pushing it with the wink, she thought. *I'd rather give you a wink than a bullet to the head.*

"So now that we got that all squared away, we have our first show in three days. As you know we have three shows in Dubai before we go to Abu Dhabi. Guys I need you to blow them away! I need rave reviews of your performance in Dubai," Jay-Roc said.

"We got you bro'!" Mouf responded. "We didn't come here to play with these niggas!"

"Facts!" Prime said in agreement.

"Get some rest, record in this beautiful studio and tomorrow we have rehearsal," Jay-Roc said. "I'm headed back to my suite. I'll see you guys tomorrow."

"I'm going to head to shorty's suite," Dirty Redd informed them before giving the guys their special Billigoat handshake. "I'll see you guys at twelve noon."

"Copy," Mouf said.

"Good night," Sparrow said in her seductive tone. "It was a pleasure seeing you again." She looked at Prime directly when she said it.

"I didn't get your name?" Prime asked.

"My name is Sarah." She licked her lips.

"The pleasure was all mine," Prime replied with equal energy.

Dirty Redd and Sparrow exited the suite headed for Sparrow's suite. As they departed, Prime was left thinking about what just took place. He would never betray his friend Dirty Redd over a woman. He had a lot of thoughts about Sparrow.

She cannot be trusted, she is up to something and it's not good. I'm going to keep an eye on her. Play her game, but I'll never really do anything with her. Let's see where this goes, Prime thought.

CHAPTER 7
CIA HEADQUARTERS, LANGLEY, VIRGINIA

Three men sat silently at the large wooden table waiting for Special Agent Heron to enter. The tension in the room was thick, partly due to the secretive nature of the meeting. Everyone knows that when you're recruited by the CIA to do a job, it's life or death.

Each man had a debt to pay for dirty deeds they were caught doing in the past. Michael 'G-Mack' Newman was a bigtime drug dealer out of Memphis, Tennessee. He started a rap record label called Get Money Records with some of his drug money. The label was a huge success until the FEDs caught G-Mack with 100 kilos of cocaine. He was facing twenty-five years to life. G-Mack's lawyer knew about secret programs run by the CIA to exonerate the felon's record. G-Mack was released to the custody of Special Agent Heron.

John 'Haitian John' Baptiste was a boss of a Haitian Cartel that ran out of Brooklyn, New York. He started off as a bodyguard for the Haitian mob boss Amos. Amos was assassinated, and Haitian John was shot four times and miraculously lived. That's how he was promoted to overlord of the Haitian Mafia.

Under John's management his crew took over territory all over the United States. They were making close to $10 million a month. They made it hot and again the FEDS arrested Haitian John and charged hm with racketeering. He was facing life in prison without the possibility of parole. Haitian John didn't know he had the same lawyer as G-Mack. That's how he was inducted into this group as well.

The third man was Captain Samuel Miller of the United States Army. Captain Miller was partners with Captain Peterson, who was in charge of the operation in Afghanistan. After the departure from United States Armed Forces, Captain Peterson retired. Captain Peterson made millions from transporting heroin to the US with Special Agent Heron, enough to buy a private island off the coast of the Virgin Islands. He handed the operation to his good friend, Captain Miller.

The huge double doors swung open, and in walked Special Agent Mike Heron wearing his signature Armani suit. He always dressed like he was a high-powered lawyer or an important businessman. He considered himself an entrepreneur, although he built his empire from smuggling heroin into the US from Afghanistan. He still thought of himself as one of the good guys.

It was like the three men all took deep breaths when he stopped at the head of the table and spoke, "Good afternoon gentlemen. You all know me as Special Agent Heron, to shorten it a bit just refer to me as Big H," Agent Heron spoke with the cockiness of a mob boss.

"What's shaking, Big H?" G-Mack was the first to speak. "You know my government name, but all my folks call me G-Mack. It's a pleasure to finally meet you in person."

"Likewise." Agent Heron shook his hand.

The other two men followed suit.

"I'm John Baptiste better known as Haitian John. Nice to meet you." He stuck his hand out for a handshake and Agent Heron obliged.

Finally, was a man dressed in full United States Army attire. He stood up stiff and saluted Agent Heron before speaking,

"Captain Samuel Miller of the First Airborne Platoon, Company B, of the United States Army." He lowered his hand from his forehead in salute to give Agent Heron a handshake. "It is a pleasure to meet you sir."

Agent Heron shook his hand. "The pleasure is all mine, Captain."

Agent Heron walked to the back of the room where there was a projector and he turned it on. There was a picture of a young Black man adorned with diamond jewelry, wearing all blue for his rolling sixties Crip gang.

"This is Derrick Holmes, also known as Young Crazy, YC for short. He is from the South side of Atlanta Georgia. He is a top member of the rolling sixties Crips. He's also a burgeoning rap artist." Agent Heron paused to let the info sink in. "We've been monitoring YC for a year, and he is the subject of our next operation." He paused to open a briefcase that contained paperwork with pictures and information and began to hand out packets to the men.

The three men in the room took the packets and examined them quickly. Each man had a specific area of expertise that was needed on the operation. "This mission is simple, yet complex. We need YC to be our new drug kingpin. The object of this operation is to supply YC with enough heroin and cocaine to take over the southern market. He will be the biggest drug dealer in the Southeast region when the mission is complete. He will also be one of the biggest rappers in the country because the CIA is getting into the music business. We'll make sure that YC becomes one of the biggest rappers at the same time we elevate him to kingpin status."

The men all shook their heads in agreement to Agent Heron's plan. Each man knew where they fit in to his plot. They just needed the instructions directly from Agent Heron. Each man was groomed for six months before this meeting. The CIA hand picks agents based on criminal history and those with exceptional skills. The CIA would hold the charges over the prospects head to persuade them into working as agents. Those with exceptional skills were often forced by the threat of killing a family member. Either way, it wasn't a pleasant situation.

"Question?" Captain Miller interjected. "Where do I come in? I know you had Colonel Peterson running the heroin from Afghanistan before the withdrawal. My operation is in South America."

Agent Heron clicked a button and a picture of a Latin man with dark hair, sharp cheek bones and full lips appeared. He looked like he could've been a model for Gucci the way he posed for the picture. This man was far from a model, he was the most feared man in South America. As soon as the picture appeared, Captain Miller knew exactly who he was.

"This is Victor Colon, also known as King Cobra. Cobra is arguably the richest and most feared man in South America due to his 100K-man drug cartel named 'Almas Perdidas,' which means Lost Souls. The Lost Souls Cartel isn't just a drug cartel; it has become a para-military brigade. They control 85 percent of the drugs smuggled out of South America, the remaining 15 percent is ours," Agent Heron spoke as if he was a scholar on the subject.

"King Cobra has been the only adversary to our efforts in South America. He refuses to do business with us. He told me himself that he would never work with the United States government," Captain Miller said nonchalantly.

Agent Heron smiled. "You're right, he has refused to do any business with the US in the past. With the new administration in charge all that has changed. King Cobra has agreed to give the US 35 percent of his share of the drug trade he imports to America, in exchange for unlimited access to the southern border of the United States."

Captain Miller sighed. "That is a direct breach of security of the United States. It's Treason, and the implications of such an act can be catastrophic. With unlimited access to the southern border, King Cobra could literally flood America with an Army."

"The terms of the agreement are for four years. We'll be monitoring how many people we allow to cross the border illegally. When the terms are up, we'll just round up all the illegal immigrants and send them home." Agent Heron clasped his hands together in a gesture of mock superiority.

Captain Miller knew when to quit. "You have it all under control. Just let me know what you need me to do on this operation."

"Your job is to smuggle the heroin and cocaine through King Cobra's pipeline directly to our new asset, YC. From there Haitian John will be the plug, as they say in the hood, to YC." Agent Heron prided himself on his extensive knowledge of street vernacular.

"I have a question," Haitian John interjected. "Is this YC dude from the South side of Atlanta?"

Agent Heron looked annoyed and confused. "Yes, that's what I said. YC is the biggest Crip on the South side of Atlanta." Agent Heron rolled his eyes and shook his head simultaneously before continuing. "Why did you ask?"

"Well, the Crips on the South side of Atlanta kind of know, or shall I say heard about me snitching. I would be committing suicide going down there," Haitian John spoke with real fear in his voice.

"We are aware of your, shall I say, rat problem in the hood. For your protection we will be monitoring YC and his crew very closely. We will inform you if they are coming for you." Agent Heron gave Haitian John a smug expression that didn't reassure him he was safe.

"Fuck it, for $200K I'll take my chances," Haitian John responded.

"Last but not least is my main man Michael G-Mack Newman. I'm a fan of the artist on your label. I play, what's his name, Dirty Lo, all the time in my Bentley. I like that line where he says, 'Killing these niggas like a roach / from coast to coast.' Man, that Dirty Lo is how they say in the hood, lit!" Agent Heron said with mock urban expression.

When G-Mack opened his mouth all you saw was white gold and VVS diamonds shining like tiny lights. "I appreciate it, playa. Dirty Lo is my top artist, he sells more records than any artist in rap today," G-Mack spoke like a proud father.

I know he's number one in the country because we have been covertly promoting that filth to make it number one, Agent Heron thought.

"It's obvious where you come in. You're going to sign YC to a contract for an unprecedented amount. We will provide you with the money for his deal and we'll be assisting to propel him from behind the scenes."

"Shit, hell yeah! That sounds like a damn good plan to me. Anytime I can goddam make some more money, I'm all in. Ya feel me?" G-Mack spoke with a signature Memphis drawl.

"If each of you will check your bank accounts, you'll see one hundred thousand dollars added to your business account from Macomb & Loeb Trust," Agent Heron instructed.

Each man took out their cell phones, went onto their banking app and immediately saw the hundred thousand from Macomb & Loeb Trust.

"You will receive another hundred thousand when the mission is complete in six months. Always keep in mind you are being listened to and watched." Agent Heron looked into each man's eyes with a dead serious expression. "You are dismissed."

The three men exited the room. That's when the back wall did a 360-degree flip and there sat a demure eighty-five-year-old man. He was well dressed in all-black from head to toe, with black horn-rimmed glasses. He stood up and slowly walked toward Agent Heron.

"Great job, Agent Heron." He shook his hand before continuing. "Do you have time for a gentleman's game of chess?"

"Of course, Director Cohen." Agent Heron pressed a button on the table, and it turned into a virtual chessboard. "I know you prefer to be black, but I want to make the game a little interesting. Allow me to be black this time."

Director Cohen smiled. "There was always a method to me being black on the chessboard. You see the white player always goes first which gives him a natural advantage. However, the skilled chess player can overcome that adversity to be the victor. Always anticipate the unexpected in any situation." Director Cohen made the first move by moving the white pawn in front of his queen.

"I set it up just like you instructed. Haitian John has no idea we already know he's a marked man in the South side of Atlanta, which will make sense when he is murdered in six months, right before he is to receive the balance." Agent Heron made a countermove with the same pawn.

"I also like the way you chose G-Mack as the label because we already have interest at his label." Director Cohen moved a second pawn that was in front of the king.

"There's another reason I chose him as well." Agent Heron moved the same pawn, mirroring Director Cohen's move. "G-Mack's main artist Dirty Lo is in a rap battle with Dirty Redd, who is signed to American D-Boy Records." He paused.

Director Cohen grinned. "I see the move; you're going to create a war between the two to cause a diversion; kind of like what we did in the early nineties with Biggie and Tupac. Very clever. By the way, how's Agent Sparrow doing on her mission?"

"She's turning out to be quite the professional if I do say so myself. She's secured a foothold into the Billigoat group getting real time intel twenty-four-seven."

"Great! Again, keep up the good work. Remember, me and you are the only ones that know about D-Boy. We made a tremendous amount of money, and there's more to be made. Need I remind you that we'll both draw a lake of fire if anyone were to find out about our international clandestine endeavors?" He paused to cough. "We are steadily moving toward our main goal. Each move is meticulous just like a game of chess. We keep the masses on the level of playing life like a game of checkers, while we move them like mere pawns on the chessboard of life." Director Cohen smiled at his own wisdom.

Agent Heron shook his head in agreement with his leader.

The two men continued playing their gentleman's game of chess quietly.

———

THE LOST SOULS COMPOUND, BOGOTÁ, COLUMBIA

The Lost Souls drug manufacturing compound was like a drug dealer's heaven. They manufactured two tons of cocaine a week. Cocaine was distributed around the world from this facility. Armed guards were stationed throughout the compound because at any time a full fledge attack from rival cartels was imminent.

King Cobra rarely visited the facility. He had Rodolfo, the second in command of his operations for that. Today he had to meet with twenty of his top soldiers to tell them about his new plan with the US government. This was the biggest deal King Cobra ever made with an adversary. What the US government didn't know was his real intension for the deal.

An all-black bullet-proof Mercedes Benz G63 pulled up in front of the main building. The driver got out and opened the door for King Cobra. He stepped out wearing an all-white linen suit with his signature dark shades. He was rushed directly into the building by the Mercedes. King Cobra had so many powerful enemies you couldn't take any risk.

He was escorted to a conference room where twenty of his most trusted soldiers were awaiting him. When he entered the room, they all stood at attention for their leader. "Please be seated," he said as he waltzed to the front of the room. "Gentlemen, we are on the brink of a new era for our organization. The days of fearing the US government are over. I have finally decided to strike a deal with the devil. They think the deal is in their favor, but I assure you it's far from that. In fact, when it's all over, Almas Perdida's will own America!"

"Yeah!" all the men yelled in unison.

"They think we're stupid, but it is they who are the dumb ones. They don't know we are going to increase our army by another 50K men and women and they'll cross the border and set up hundreds of small businesses we will control. They won't even know what hit them. In four years, our organization will amass so much of the American's wealth that it will cripple their economy, leaving us as the ruling class!"

"Yeah!" the men yelled again in unison.

"No longer will South America be second to America! We will be the richest among those arrogant Americans. We will show them we are not wetback spics, but that we are Latin Kings!" King Cobra raised his fist in the air. "Larga Vida a las almas Perdidas!"

"Larga Vida a las almas Perdidas!" the men yelled back in unison.

"Each one of you will receive a $10K increase in your pay when we start the takeover."

"King Cobra! King Cobra! King Cobra!" the men shouted to the top of their lungs.

"After we take over America, we will take over the world."

CHAPTER 8
AL MAJAZ AMPHITHEATER, AL SHARJAH, UAE

Dirty Redd laughed as he watched the video on his phone. "You see this dirty little boy trying to get points off me? I'm the original Dirty and he mad because he can't fuck with me!" Dirty Redd ranted to his fellow Billigoats.

"Fuck that scumbag!" Prime chimed in. "He don't really want no smoke!"

"That's what I'm talking about!" Dirty Redd gave Prime a solid handshake.

"Fuck that bitch ass nigga! This is the last show in the United Arab Emirates, then it's back to the states. Let's leave them with a long-lasting impression they'll never forget," Mouf said as the Billigoats gathered in their pre-show huddle. "Dirty, I'm proud of you for stepping up on these shows. I appreciate you, brother." Mouf gave Dirty Redd a brotherly hug.

"No doubt, king, you know how we do. I couldn't have done it without you, my nigga," Dirty Redd responded.

Sparrow stood right by Dirty Redd's side for the whole tour. They had become quite the item, showing affection in public. Even the tabloids were talking about the two love birds. It promoted Dirty Redd, which they used to promote the clothing line. Since they started the UAE tour, Billigoat clothing did a 25 percent increase in sales.

Prime was always eyeing Sparrow from his peripheral and she knew it. He still held on to his hunch that Sparrow a.k.a. Sarah, was up to something. She was on to his suspicion, so these last two weeks she kept it low and hadn't reported to Agent Heron in the same amount of time. She knew she had to report soon, or risk being reprimanded, which could mean possible termination.

When they go on stage I'll check in with Agent Heron, Sparrow thought.

"On three! One, two, three! Billigoats rule!" all three of the men shouted before heading to the stage.

As they were about to go on stage, Sparrow strolled back toward the dressing room. Prime saw her and decided to double back to the dressing room before she got there.

"Where are you going?" Dirty Redd asked.

"I have to use the bathroom!" Prime shouted back.

Prime dashed, while Sparrow strolled, at the same time she took out her phone to call Agent Heron. Prime was able to beat her to the dressing room. He hid between some clothes on a portable rack. He positioned himself so he could peep through the clothes.

"I have it all under control. He has no idea what I'm about to drop on his head." Sparrow was on a video call when she entered the room. "After his show, I'm going to tell him I'm pregnant. That'll get him excited enough for me to tighten my grip."

"Good direction switch. That way he'll feel obligated to you over everyone who opposes his 'baby mama'," Agent Heron added his touch of ghetto vernacular for the effect.

"This is the last show in the UAE. From here we're back in the states," Sparrow added.

"Any sign of D-Boy?" Agent Heron asked.

"There are two strange Arab guys that got on the tour in

Dubai. They pose no threat, there's something about them that I can't put my finger on just yet. But they are on my radar."

"I need their full names and a picture of them both ASAP. You know protocol, why didn't you report this two weeks ago when the tour started?" Agent Heron asked vehemently.

"Apologies sir, it'll never happen again. I got caught up in securing my asset and I lost track of time," Sparrow responded with humility.

"Don't let this happen again."

Prime peeped through the clothes and saw Agent Heron's face while he was talking. He could hear every word in the conversation. He couldn't believe what he was hearing.

I knew this bitch was a fucking spy or something. If she thinks she's going to play my brother like that she has another thing coming.

Prime was fuming at the thought of what he was hearing. He accidentally moved and Sparrow looked in his direction. At first glance she didn't see him, but upon further examination she saw the shape of a person. Prime peeped through the clothes and that's when Sparrow saw him. She stared right into the slit of clothing Prime was peering through.

"You can come out, I see you," Sparrow said as she walked closer to the clothes rack. "I know what you're thinking. It's not what it sounds like."

"What it sound like then?" Prime asked as he came from the midst of the clothing rack to reveal himself. "It sounds like you have some fucking explaining to do. I heard the whole conversation. What the fuck, I mean who the fuck are you?" Prime asked with spite.

"Listen, I'm an investigative reporter doing a story on the Billigoats," Sparrow explained nonchalantly as she inched closer to Prime.

"No, fuck that! I heard you say you're going to put a baby on him. That isn't no damn investigative reporting, that's some I-spy shit and I'm not letting my boy go out like that." Prime made his way to the door.

Just as he was about to grab the door handle Sparrow yelled, "Wait! Can we work something out?"

Prime stopped in his tracks and turned to face her. "Work it out like how? 'Cause if you think you can seduce me—" Prime's last words were cut off by a swift chop to his larynx which caused him to grab his throat with both hands while he gurgled.

"I see we have a failure to communicate," Sparrow said sarcastically, noticing his inability to speak.

She took the palm of her hand and did an upper thrust to Prime's nose bone so powerful it punctured his frontal lobe. His brain began to hemorrhage immediately. Prime fell to the ground and within ten seconds he was brain dead. All it took was another minute and he would be pronounced clinically dead.

"Oh, look at Prime. You just couldn't mind your business, now look at you." Sparrow looked him in his eyes while they still had life. "I tried to work it out with you but no, you had to take the high road. Now you're on the highway to heaven. Sweet dreams." She manually closed his eyes and exited the dressing room.

Sparrow began to run frantically through the backstage hall-way. "Oh my God!" she screamed, "Somebody help me! Prime is dead!" she said to a police officer standing guard by the stage. "Prime is dead!"

"Calm down, miss!" the officer said. "Who is Prime?" He had no idea who she was talking about.

"The Billigoat, Prime. He's dead in the dressing room."

He understood, so he sprang into action, calling in the crime on his radio receiver. "We have a possible homicide in the Billigoats dressing room."

When they reached the dressing room, Prime had globs of blood streaming from his nose. It was evident he was dead. It was a gory scene that the officer couldn't bear to watch, so he turned his head and closed his eyes. Sparrow just stared at Prime as if this was just a day at the office.

When the officer opened his eyes, Sparrow pretended to be nauseous, and she ran to the bathroom at the back of the room. She quickly took out her cell phone and called Agent Heron.

"We have a small problem. I just killed Prime," Sparrow stated with a hint of panic.

"Why did you kill him?" Agent Heron asked in a calm tone.

"He was hiding in a clothes rack the whole time we were talking. He heard everything."

"How could you get caught slipping like that? You didn't secure the area before communicating? Obviously not." Agent Heron was a bit perturbed at the news.

"I didn't, sir. He was able to double back and hide himself before I entered the dressing room," Sparrow explained.

"What's done is done. I'm going to send a cleanup crew to cover your ass. Agent Sparrow, you know the agency doesn't tolerate screw ups. Don't let this happen again or, well you know." Agent Heron hung up the phone.

When she exited the bathroom Mouf, and Dirty Redd were both standing over Prime's lifeless body crying hysterically. She had to get into character, so she swiftly let tears run down her face and she ran to Dirty Redd.

"I'm the one that found his body," she said while crying a river of tears.

"Who fucking did this?" Dirty Redd yelled. "My brother is gone, man!" streams of tears ran down Dirty Redd's face. Sparrow held him.

Mouf covered his eyes with his hand trying to maintain his emotions. "I can't believe this is happening."

Jay-Roc, D-Boy, and John were the last to enter the room to see Prime laying there dead. John immediately went into agent mode. He had seen this type of attack before. He knelt so he was eye level with Prime's forehead.

"This was done by a professional," John made the mistake of speaking in his regular voice and Sparrow quickly noticed it.

This guy isn't Arab. Who is he, Sparrow thought.

The small crowd was broken up by police officers and EMS workers coming to haul Prime's body off to the local morgue. Through the small sea of officers and workers came Detectives Muhammad and Bashir. They had been assigned to keep an eye on the Billigoats's tour.

As John looked up from examining Prime's wound, he saw Muhammad and Bashir coming toward him. It was too late to hide from them, so he faced them directly.

"What a pleasant surprise," John said in his mock Arab accent. "We meet again."

"Rahman is it?" Bashir asked cynically. "Fancy meeting you here."

"You know what they say, Rahman?" Muhammad asked.

"They, who is they, and what do they say?" John kept up the sarcasm to throw them off. He knew this was an emergency.

John's wittiness frustrated Detective Bashir. "They is the people, and if it walks like a camel, it's not a duck." Detective Bashir was flustered when he spoke.

This just keeps getting more interesting by the minute, Sparrow thought as she watched the exchange between John and the Arab detectives.

"Stop with the double-talk and riddles, you are now part of an active investigation. Detain this man!" Detective Bashir demanded.

"Detain me for what? I wasn't even in the vicinity of this crime and there are at least twenty witnesses that can attest to that including that officer." John pointed to the officer that Sarah stopped.

"He is telling the truth. She was the first to encounter the body." The officer pointed toward Sarah.

There were too many people around so Agents Bashir and

Mohammed couldn't flex their muscle on John. John felt the energy shift in his direction, so he took advantage of the situation.

"It seems as if you two rogue agents always end up wherever I am. It doesn't take a genius to figure out that you are following me and now you're showing up and there's a dead body. For all we know, you murdered Prime," John said defiantly.

Everyone looked at the two agents as suspects because John had a point. The first person to respond was the officer on the scene. "Can you show me your credentials? You said you were agents of what agency?"

Both agents pulled out badges that read *Bureau of Special Investigation, Abu Dubai, United Arab Emirates.* The officer examined the badges and returned them immediately. The agents put the badges back into their back pockets, then looked at John.

"You're lucky this time, Rahman, but if there ever is another time you are at a crime scene, don't consider yourself so lucky," Agent Bashir said as he and Agent Mohammed took charge of the scene.

D-Boy kept his distance from the agents. D-Boy was still street minded when it came to the police. It was a habit he acquired from the years he spent selling drugs on the street. He was also cautious because of his situation as a fugitive.

Dirty Redd was in visible pain from finding his best friend dead. Sarah was hugging him to console him. She was whispering into his ear, "It's going to be alright, baby."

Part of her felt bad for being the cause of his pain. The other side of her was coldhearted and didn't care about his life either way. She was a trained assassin, so her emotions were in check. Now it was just a matter of her continuing the facade with Dirty Redd and completing her mission.

Jay-Roc was stoic. He showed no emotion. He was just shaking his head at the sight of Prime laying there with blood gushing from his nose. A group of officers showed up and they were canvassing and roping off the area.

"Excuse me, but you all must step away from the crime scene so we can do our job," Agent Mohammad asked politely.

The small crowd stepped away from Prime's body while an officer corded off the area with yellow tape. As he moved back from Prime's body, Dirty Redd hugged Mouf while crying hysterically. Mouf was fighting back tears that won their battle, because the tears streamed down his face as if a dam had broken. Mouf was the leader of the trio, he took it harder than expected. Prime and Mouf became close by default. Prime and Dirty Redd had known each other since the first grade, however Prime and Mouf got closer because Dirty Redd was always the one messing things up for the group.

"I can't believe this is happening, Prime is fucking dead!" Mouf said breaking the silence.

"The question is who the fuck did this to him?" Jay-Roc asked getting looks from Dirty Redd and Mouf. "Whoever did this is probably still in the area. We went on stage and five minutes later Prime is dead!"

"I asked him where he was going, and he just said he had to use the bathroom before we went on stage. Next thing I know he's dead with no explanation," Dirty Redd said through a stream of tears.

"Whoever did this had a motive. No one kills a person like this without a motive," Mouf stated.

"That's the problem. Prime didn't have any beef or serious enemies that would want him dead. Especially here in the UAE," Jay-Roc responded.

Sarah did her best innocent act. She stayed behind Dirty Redd rubbing on his back while they talked. She tried not to make eye contact with anyone, but she couldn't help but notice John was occasionally looking at her suspiciously. It was the same way Prime started to look at her before she killed him.

John was highly trained by the Israeli Intelligence Agency known as the Massad. It is custom for every Israeli citizen to join the Israeli Army, it's optional to join the Intelligence Agency. John opted to join the Massad after his best friend, Ira, influenced him to sign up. Ira was killed in a sting operation, and that's when John resigned and became a lawyer.

From his training, John could tell the killer was stealth because they didn't leave a trace of evidence. He knew this was the work of another trained agent. He saw the way Prime's nose bone punctured his brain. Pieces of Prime's brain matter were leaking through his nostrils.

This is a classic death kill move of a highly skilled assassin. The only people that were around us this whole time I took the time to do a background check on, except the girl, John thought.

John glanced over at Sarah, and she caught eye contact with him again. She didn't turn away suspiciously, she just shed tears and wiped them away with the back of her hand. She hid her face in her hands hoping that John wasn't still looking at her when she lowered them. When she lowered her hands, John had moved from her sight.

Two EMS workers made their way through the crowd pushing a gurney. "Excuse us! Coming through!"

They stopped at Prime's body, professionally placed him in a body bag and zipped it up. They lifted him onto the gurney and made their way back through the small crowd to the ambulance. They put his body in the vehicle and drove off.

Jay-Roc had to take control of the situation. "Listen up! This is an unexpected tragedy, but we must keep it on the low until we get out of here. This was the last show in the UAE, tomorrow we're back in the states."

"Back in the states without Prime. What are we going to tell his daughters and his parents? That he got murdered and we have no idea who did it and why!" Dirty Redd said through a river of tears.

"I know. We still have to keep it together. For Prime, for the team," Jay-Roc stated with surety.

"He's right. Prime would've wanted us to be strong in his absence. Let's get on this flight back to the states and represent our brother Prime. You'll never be forgotten," Mouf said defiantly.

D-Boy and John glanced at each other at that statement of going back to the states. They both waited seven years for this moment, and now it was finally happening. They were going home, back to America. Although Prime's death was a proverbial rain on their parade, they were still elated about going home.

"I feel like Eddie Murphy in *Coming to America*," D-Boy said to John, accidentally using his New York accent. Sarah heard it.

Sarah was moving around the scene inconspicuously, so D-Boy and John didn't notice her in the vicinity. No one else caught the slip of the accent from D-Boy besides Sarah. She stayed in the perimeter of their conversation waiting to hear D-Boy say more so she could confirm what she heard. She used Dirty Redd as a shield to hide herself from John and D-Boy as they spoke.

I knew something was fishy about these two, she thought.

"I just scheduled an early take off in the jet. That's what I spend all this money for," Jay-Roc said.

"Good move," Dirty Redd said in response to Jay-Roc's command.

D-Boy spoke out of character from the Arab he was disguised as, Dirty Redd didn't catch it but Sarah and John caught the slip of D-Boy's accent. John nudged D-Boy and Sarah noticed it. At the same time John caught eye contact with Sarah, and they had a mind readers moment where they both understood what just happened. Sarah just smiled at him knowing that this time she heard his New York accent clear as day. So did John.

"Let's blow this popsicle stand. Say goodbye to Dubai, we're out of here." Jay -Roc moved and eight people moved with him, minus one.

They all drove in the Mercedes Benz sprinter on the way to the private et. They rushed onto the jet single file. Everyone quickly chose a seat. John calculated his seat to be in front of Sarah and Dirty Redd's seats. As they got comfortable and ready for takeoff, John looked at Sarah and smiled.

"Greetings, I'm Rahman. I didn't get your name," John said in his fake Arab accent.

"My name is Sarah," she said with a sinister smile.

"Where are you from my dear? Let me guess. If I had to suppose I'd say you're from the Mid-West," John asked in a friendly manner, watching every motion with a microscope.

"You are absolutely right. I'm from Milwaukee, Wisconsin," Sarah answered truthfully.

John looked at her hands. "May I read your palms?"

"Yo, Jay! What's up with your man's and the twenty-one questions? You're giving me weird vibes with this palm reading act! Next, you're going to be casting spells or some shit!" Dirty Redd said with angry sarcasm.

"No, it's okay, I love palm readings," Sarah said in curiosity of John's request.

John gently grabbed her hands and noticed the slightly bruised lower half of her palm where she hit Prime's nose bone with enough thrust to puncture his brain with it. A blow that powerful was bound to cause an injury to her palm. He looked at her palms then he used his thumb to rub over the bruise with just enough pressure to cause Sarah to wince.

She snatched her hand from him as a reflex. "Did I do something wrong?" John asked, mock perplexing his action.

I know exactly what's wrong with your palm. You used it to kill Prime, John thought to himself.

"No, I just don't want to get my palms read now. No big deal," Sarah said, trying to deflect the situation.

"Okay, but maybe next time. Anyone else up for a palm reading?" John asked.

"Bro' come on, enough with the bullshit! I just lost my best friend and you're over here doing fucking palm readings! Who is this guy anyway?" Dirty Redd asked in anger.

"Apologies, I was only trying to lighten the situation with entertainment," John answered humbly.

"It's alright, Rahman. Dirty didn't mean anything by it. We're all dealing with Prime's killing the best way we can," Jay-Roc said, injecting peace into the conversation.

The exchange was interrupted by a voice over the intercom. "This is your captain speaking, please fasten your seatbelts and get ready for takeoff."

Sarah and John caught eye contact one last time before the doors shut and the jet taxied down the runway headed for JFK airport in New York.

CHAPTER 9
JFK AIRPORT QUEENS, NEW YORK

"Please fasten your seatbelts, we'll land in about ten minutes. I hope you enjoyed your flight," the pilot announced.

Dirty Redd looked out of the window at the New York City skyline. "Home sweet home."

"Word! It feels good to be back in New York, baby!" Mouf said.

D-Boy was resting, that's when John tapped him on the shoulder. "Wake up sleepy head, we're about to land." He made sure he was in character when he spoke. They couldn't afford any slip ups.

D-Boy immediately woke up and peered out of the window at the skyline. "I thought the Dubai skyline was beautiful, but this is magnificent!" he spoke in the accent he was trained to speak with. After slipping up at the concert, he made sure he was on point with his character.

"I've been to New York several times, so this is but another trip to the Big Apple as they call it in the states." John got into lockstep with D-Boy as an Arab.

Sarah was looking out of her window pretending not to be listening to them for the slightest hint of deception. She was already suspicious because of the palm reading debacle. She knew Rahman wasn't a fool, and he was more than he led on to be.

I must get more intel on these two to report back to Agent Heron. I need to get them into the federal databank to see just exactly who they really are. I have a hunch something is up with them, Sarah thought as she made her way to the restroom.

"Hey babe, I'm going to use the bathroom," Sarah said after kissing Dirty Redd on his cheek.

When she was out of earshot, D-Boy pulled John to the side. "What was that palm reading skit about? You have to let me know what's going on in your mind sometimes, so I'll know you're not just losing it."

"I think she killed Prime. She smells like an agent. Whoever killed Prime was with us. Prime and Sarah were the only ones alone before he wound up dead. I faked like I was reading her palm to see if it was bruised in the precise location consistent with the type of blow that would've done that damage," John spoke like an expert.

D-Boy gave John a serious look. "You remind me of a modern-day Sherlock Holmes sometimes. So, you're telling me that shorty, Sarah, killed a grown man with her fucking palm?" He found this hard to believe.

"It's a classic assassin's technique that every Intelligence Agency teaches in basic training. It's what we refer to in the intelligence community as a DKB short for 'Death Kill Blow' tactic. If I'm correct, she's in the bathroom calling her superior as we speak," John spoke nonchalantly as he quickly assessed that Dirty Redd was speaking to Mouf. "Just like I'm certain that Dirty Redd is talking to Mouf about us this very moment."

D-Boy turned his head a little and he quickly glanced at them in the distance. "You're right. Why aren't you going after Sarah before she contacts her superior?"

"I want her to so she can run into a brick wall. Our identity's our sealed tight. Not even the CIA can penetrate it," John answered matter-of-factly.

Dirty Redd and Mouf were standing thirty feet from John and D-Boy speaking and occasionally peering over at them. Dirty Redd was developing a disdain for them.

"Something about these Arab dudes, what's their names?" Dirty Redd asked Mouf with a scowl on his face.

"I think his name is Rahman and the other dude is Mustafa. I'm good with names. I always want to know who's around me. Especially some new ass foreign niggas," Mouf responded.

"Facts, that's what the fuck I'm saying! They could be Muslim terrorist for all we know. The way the nigga grabbed my shorty hand talking about, 'Can I read your palm?' I wanted to smack the shit out the nigga," Dirty Redd said with malice.

"Where did your girl go?" Mouf asked noticing her absence.

"She went to the bathroom. That Arab dude did something to her hand when he touched her palm. She snatched her hand back in pain, that's why I got a little mad."

"I saw that. It looked like he squeezed her hand and she let out a noise like she was in pain. I thought I was bugging," Mouf responded.

"You weren't bugging, this fucking dude did something that caused her to flinch in pain. Plus, the fact that Prime is dead. I can't believe he's dead. This is crazy!" Dirty Redd looked directly at John and shook his head.

John just responded with a kowtow, as a show of respect, but it didn't work. Dirty Redd rolled his eyes at John and turned away. John knew he had to move very subtly around Dirty Redd. He didn't want him investigating the situation and finding out something he shouldn't know.

INSIDE THE FEMALE'S **BATHROOM**

Sarah walked in and inspected the bathroom to make sure the coast was clear before she called Agent Heron. She then locked the door so no one could enter. She put her back against the wall and took a deep breath. She needed to decompress from all the drama that happened in the last twenty-four hours.

This is crazy! I didn't want to kill Prime, I had to. Now I have to watch out for Rahman because I have a feeling he squeezed my palm for a reason. He knew something. I'm not going to jump to conclusions, I just need to get this intel to Agent Heron, she thought to herself before calling Agent Heron.

She pressed call. While the phone rang, she took three deep breaths before Agent Heron answered.

"Well, if it isn't my favorite female agent, Sparrow. What do you have for me today?" Agent Heron said gleefully.

"I have good news and bad news."

"Let me get the bad news first," Agent Heron asked.

"The bad news is that after I killed Prime one of the Arab guys noticed the bruise on my palm. I'm not sure but I think he is a foreign diplomat or something. I need to check his identity on the federal data bank to insure he is who he says he is," Sarah said through measured breaths. She was always nervous when she spoke to Agent Heron.

"What about the other Arab guy. How does he check out?"

"I want to run them both in the databank. The other guy seemed okay, but I did detect a glitch in his accent. As if he was purposely speaking like an Arab for a quick second. I could be wrong. I still need to run him, too."

"What's the good news?"

"I made it back to the United States in one piece. After killing Prime, I thought I had to stay for the investigation because I was the one that found his body," Sara answered.

"I get it. How were you able to get out of the country so fast without being questioned?" Agent Heron asked curiously.

"Jay-Roc just told his pilot he was ready to go, and the jet was ready for us to take off when we got there."

"I see, the privilege of having money and power. Good thing he was able to get you out of there because if they were to detain you that would be bad news."

"So, my next move is to claim I'm pregnant to get closer to Dirty Redd emotionally."

"I thought you did that already?" Agent Heron asked.

"I waited a little bit. Now is the right time because it will distract him from the killing of his best friend," she explained.

"Okay, good job, Sparrow. Send me photos of the two Arabs so I can do a facial recognition scan on them as well as a federal background check," Agent Heron stated.

"I do not have any photos of them yet, give me a couple of days to submit them. Their names on the manifest are Rahman Muhammed and Mustafa Bengali of Dubai, United Arab Emirates." Sarah was sidetracked by a woman knocking on the door.

"Hey, I need to use the bathroom! You've been in there for the longest!" the woman yelled.

"I'll be out in a second," Sarah responded. "I have to go. Is there anything else?"

"That will be all for now. I'll contact you when I need to. Keep up the good work, Agent Sparrow." She disconnected the phone and exited the stall.

When she exited the bathroom, Dirty Redd and Mouf were standing nearby. Sarah had a worried look on her face as she approached Dirty Redd. She made it obvious that something was troubling her. She knew with all the excitement and the murder of his best friend what she was about to allude to might be too much.

"What's wrong with you? Why do you look like you lost your best friend?" Dirty Redd asked, noticing her demeanor.

"Well, I was expecting my period like three days ago. I'm not going to jump to conclusions though." Sarah frowned.

"I don't know how to take that. I mean part of me is happy because one life was taken, and one was given." Dirty Redd was known to be philosophical.

She smiled. "That's a relief, because I thought you were just going to be totally opposed to it being that we just met."

"I'm feeling you, so it's just I'm still mourning Prime's death. I still can't believe he's dead." He shed tears and hugged Sarah.

Sarah held Dirty Redd and closed her eyes. When she opened them, Rahman was looking right into her eyes for a split second. She felt the coldness in his stare. She continued with her role as consoling girlfriend, as she rubbed Dirty Redd's back and whispered consoling words in his ear.

"It'll be alright, baby. Just let it out. It's okay."

The touching moment was interrupted by Jay-Roc. "Alright everybody let's get on the sprinter so we can get back to our lives for a couple of days. I postponed two dates so we can bury Prime. This is hitting the Hip-Hop world hard so let's lay low for a week, then we're back at it."

Everyone shook their heads in agreement and moved onto the sprinter as instructed. When they were on the sprinter, Sarah glanced over at Rahman. He just smiled. Dirty Redd noticed the exchange and scowled at Rahman. Mouf noticed the exchange and looked over at Mustafa. All the while no one said a word. They all just drove in silence thinking about the one person that wasn't there.

"Rest in peace my nigga, Prime," Dirty Redd said into the air.

No one replied, they all just rode in silence with their own memories of the fallen soldier.

———

KING COBRA'S **HEAVILY GUARDED MANSION, BOGOTÁ, COLUMBIA**

King Cobra sat on the plush white zebra skinned sofa watching the most important game of the year, Columbia versus Mexico. This was a longtime rivalry between the two countries. This was bigger than a game of soccer or football as they call it. This was war.

Every year King Cobra financed Columbia's national team with $2.2 million. He owned 25 percent of the team and whenever they lost, he took it very personally. So personal that he had five team members dismembered for botching a game once.

"Senior, your private line is ringing," one of his servants announced.

"Can you please bring it to me? I can't miss a second of this game. But I'll take it because I know who it is," King Cobra replied. "I've been waiting on this call from Mr. Heron all week, now he decides to call on this most important occasion," he spoke to his right-hand, Rodolfo.

"You know Americans don't care about football unless it's their version of it," Rodolfo replied.

The servant came back holding an old school, handheld, landline phone. This was the most secure phone line because there's no way to infiltrate it. Rodolfo looked at King Cobra before he answered the line. He knew the importance of this call.

"Are you ready?" Rodolfo asked with a serious tone.

"As ready as I'll ever be." King Cobra took a deep breath before answering. "Mr. Heron your timing could've been delayed. However, I hope you satisfy my patience, which I have very little of."

"You know patience is a virtue, Mr. Cobra. I never got use to the whole *king* thing," Agent Heron responded sarcastically. "Sorry for the delay, a few important matters came up that pushed back our initial start date."

"You do know that every day this project is delayed, I'm losing thousands of dollars," King Cobra informed Heron

"I do understand. That's why today I'm keeping my end of the bargain. As of today, you have confirmation that you can enter the border at the precise coordinates that I'll be sending you." Heron emailed the exact location of entry where the Lost Souls Cartel would come into America with drugs and soldiers, uninterrupted for four years.

Rodolfo looked at the tablet that received the information and confirmed exactly where it was on a GPS app. "I got it!" He smiled at King Cobra.

"It was a pleasure doing business with you, Mr. Heron." King Cobra took another deep breath to compose himself from the rush of excitement he was feeling.

"The pleasure is all mine, Mr. Cobra." Agent Heron smiled. "Before I hang up, a man by the name of Captain Miller is going to call you."

As Heron hung up, Captain Miller called. "This is Captain Miller of the United States Army. You will be taking your orders from me from this point on. Understood?" Captain Miller hated the Lost Souls Cartel. He didn't want to work with them, but he was forced.

"Whatever, you'll be working with my Lieutenant Rodolfo." King Cobra handed the phone to Rodolfo and focused on the game.

Columbia scored the winning point and the crowd erupted into a frenzy. "We did it! We won!" Rodolfo yelled in excitement. He hugged King Cobra, who was more excited about the call from Agent Heron.

"Hello," Captain Miller couldn't hear anything but cheering.

"We won the World Cup, and the Lost Souls Cartel will take over the world!" Tears streamed down King Cobra's face as he spoke.

Captain Miller hung up. "Fuck Columbia and the World Cup!" he said to himself once they were off the line.

"I just received the first location. The first convoy is ready to move. All I have to do is send them the location and it's done," Rodolfo reported.

"Send them the location, the takeover is upon you, America." King Cobra wiped the tears from his face with the back of his hand.

Rodolfo sent the location to Captain Diaz in charge of the movement of the first group of 2K soldiers. There were ten buses with 200 soldiers seated on each bus waiting on an unsecured stretch of the border near Del Rio, Texas. With the assistance of Agent Heron and the Central Intelligence Agency, the Lost Souls Cartel of Bogotá Columbia released the first wave of 50K soldiers into American territory. Once they reach Texas they will be taken to a cattle ranch. From there they would get their instructions of what city they would be shipped to. There they would set up multiple businesses in the name of the Lost Souls Cartel.

MEXICAN BORDER NEAR DEL RIO, TEXAS

Captain Diaz got the text he'd been waiting on from Rodolfo. It was difficult to see his smile because of his thick handlebar mustache. Captain Diaz was a throwback to the Columbian men of old, tough, die-hard Columbian nationalist. To Diaz, this was the moment he lived all his fifty-four years on earth for.

"Move it! Let's go!" Captain Diaz shouted over a bullhorn.

The men were outside their designated bus chatting and passing the time waiting for instructions. They all began to move in unison like a colony of ants. Quickly the men boarded their assigned bus, and within minutes the convoy was moving toward its destination, Del Rio Texas.

Captain Diaz was in the first bus sitting next to the driver. He pulled out his phone and looked at the GPS. It indicated that the ranch on the Del Rio Texas side was approximately fifty-six minutes from their hideaway spot in Mexico. They drove at a moderate speed of sixty-five miles per hour through a dirt road off the main highway.

Each soldier had a suitcase in the cargo space of their designated bus. The suitcase had five outfits, an automatic weapon and $100K in cash. Each soldier was allotted 150 rounds of ammunition, which was also in the cargo.

The caravan snaked its way through the border and in no time, they were parking the buses in a huge hanger style garage on a 300-acre cattle ranch that was also owned by King Cobra. The soldiers all exited the buses, grabbed their luggage and entered the huge main house to eat and rest.

Captain Diaz waited 'til everyone was settled before reporting back to Rodolfo. "Everything is a go, all the men are settled in and awaiting their next instructions."

"Excellent, Captain Diaz! At exactly nine a.m. you will receive instructions for each man individually," Rodolfo answered with confidence.

"Copy! I'll be ready for the transmission." Captain Diaz hung up the phone. "Viva la Columbia!"

Captain Diaz lit up a cigar and took a swig of tequila before waltzing into the main house. He passed two of his most trusted soldiers, Fernando and Diego. He handpicked and trained them both. Fernando was Diaz's nephew, his brother Alejandro's son. Diego was an orphan that became Fernando's best friend. Alejandro died in a shoot-out with a rival cartel. Diaz raised Fernando and Diego and groomed them into fearless killing machines for the Lost Souls Cartel.

"I heard there's so much money in America you can find pennies laying around in the street and on the floor. And no one stops to pick them up. Can you believe that?" Fernando said to Diego.

"Wow! An American penny is COP 3.08 in Columbia!" Diego responded.

"Just think, between us we have $200K American dollars. If we were to,"

"You two need to rest up, we're moving out from here at nine a.m. after everyone receives their instructions," Diaz commanded.

"I know, Tio, I'm just excited and I can't rest," Fernando responded.

"Me, too," Diego added. "It still hasn't hit me yet. We're in America to build the Lost Souls Cartel into an empire!"

"That's the spirit, but if you're not properly rested how are you going to be awake to absorb the information?" Diaz asked.

"You're right, Tio. I'm going to turn it in," Fernando said.

"Good night, Tio," Diego recognized Diaz as his uncle as well.

Diaz exited the room. That's when Fernando took the opportunity to whisper, "I have a plan that will make us both multimillionaires of our own cartel. Once we get to our assigned state I'll tell you." Fernando winked his eye.

Diego winked his eye in unison, confirming that he wasn't opposed to the idea of them starting their own cartel.

CHAPTER 10
JOHNSON'S FUNERAL HOME, SOUTHSIDE JAMAICA QUEENS

Prime's funeral was one fit for a king. It was like the entire NYC came out to say farewell to Benjamin Hudson, better known as the rap star Prime. This was an unexpected turn of events for the young burgeoning artist. He was only twenty-eight years old. He was just starting to understand life and it was taken from him.

Prime had three kids from three different women, and they were all in attendance. As were four other women claiming to be Prime's woman. Prime became quite the lady's man after his rise to fame. He was already getting women, but after the success of the Billigoats, his female attraction was off the meter. Jay-Roc said he gets more fan mail and emails asking about Prime than Mouf and Dirty Redd put together.

The whole American D-Boy staff sat in the first two rows with Prime's family. Mouf and Dirty Redd wore dark glasses hiding their crying eyes from the public. Sarah sat beside Dirty Redd pretending to mourn for the man she murdered. She felt a spec of pity for his children, other than that her heart was cold as ice about her actions. She was trained that way, so she was just going with the flow. She rubbed Dirty Redd's back to show some compassion for his loss.

There was a big picture of Prime on a stand. There was no

casket, Prime wished to be cremated. His oldest son's mother had his last will and testament, so she presented it to the funeral home. Prime's philosophy was that funerals are expensive. He didn't want to lay the burden on his family to have a lavish burial.

"We will take this time to ask anyone that has a kind word to say about Benjamin to please feel free to come up," the funeral attendant said on the microphone that was attached to a podium.

Mouf and Dirty Redd walked up together, Dirty Redd took the podium first. "Peace. I usually have a lot to say, but today I'm at a loss for words. I never would have imagined in 100 years that this would happen to my brother. We grew up together since we were twelve years old, we've always had each other's back. The day..." he paused to compose himself. "The day he was murdered he was so full of life and happiness. Anyone that knows Prime knows that he is the positive light of any room he steps in. He was the peacemaker of the group, he never let us fight without intervening. My condolences go out to his children and their mothers. That's all I have to say." Dirty Redd stood aside so Mouf could take the podium.

"I'm not a big talker, so I'm going to be short." He cleared his throat. "I didn't know Prime as long as Dirty Redd did. However, we became just as close in a short amount of time. He was my brother, we were closer than my real brother. He kept me grounded when I would go off the path. I'm going to miss you brother." Mouf wiped his tears and walked away from the podium.

A few more people came to the podium to speak. Afterward there was a gathering with food and refreshments. That's when John made eye contact with Sarah. They locked their eyes, each waiting for the other to give in and look away. Sarah didn't look away, she stared coldly into John's eyes. If looks could kill, John would've died stiff on the spot.

Dirty Redd caught the staring match. "What the fuck are you

looking at?" he said to John.

"Apologies, I meant no harm." John did a kowtow.

"Whatever, just stay the fuck away from my girl!" Dirty Redd grabbed her hand and led her out of the funeral home. Mouf accompanied him.

"What's with you and Dirty Redd?" Jay-Roc asked John.

"Not sure, but I think it has something to do with his girl, Sarah," John responded.

"Dirty is just going through it. Him and Prime were very close. Don't take it personal," Jay-Roc said.

"I won't." John grabbed a bottle of water and sipped it.

———

SOUTHSIDE ATLANTA, GEORGIA

YC and five of the most trusted members of his gang were smoking back-to-back blunts. The smoke filled the living room area of the abandoned house, formally known as the 'bando'. They turned it into a $10K a week drug operation and only stayed two months before they moved on to the next bando. They were able to dodge the narcs, the snitches, and the jack boys.

YC was only twenty-one years old, but he moved like a seasoned veteran on the streets. His father, Jaybird, was one of the biggest drug dealers on the Southside of Atlanta. He ran a million-dollar a year drug operation. YC was Jaybird's only son, he taught him everything he knew about the streets.

"You always have to stick and move out here in these streets. Never stay in one spot longer than two months, that'll keep all your enemies off guard. Always remember—" Jaybird was cut off by his then sixteen-year-old son.

"I know, keep your friends close, but your enemies closer. You only have brothers, your friends will fry you in the end. Test your brother's loyalty, anyone that proves to be disloyal should

be disposed of immediately!" Young YC quoted Jaybird like a street scholar.

Jaybird was killed in a robbery when YC was sixteen, that's how he got the name Young Crazy. After his father was murdered he went insane. He killed five people because he heard they might've had something to do with his father's death. His father was his hero, he lived and breathed his essence. Not only did YC resemble his father, but he also had his temperament and demeanor. YC was not to be fucked with.

YC's new song was playing. "Yo, this shit hitting!" said Cheese, YC's second in command. "Bro' if the DJs don't bang this a thousand times them niggas don't know good music."

YC gave him their gang's signature handshake before speaking. "Good looking, bro'. When I get on with this music shit I'm bringing you with me every step of the way. You the reason I do that shit for real. You kept telling me I was nice with the shit, so I kept going," YC explained.

"Now look, people are taking you seriously. Every time you drop a video you get 100K views the first day. That's major!" Cheese said with vigor.

Mel, another member chimed in, "Facts! I heard your music blasting out of this Range Rover yesterday. Buddy was bopping his head crazy to your joint!"

"Now is the time to get this deal to promote you to the top!" Cheese said.

"I can't quit my day job, know what I mean? That rap shit is fun, I like to do it in my spare time. Until I see a check, I'm not trying to be a fucking rapper for real," YC replied.

"I feel you, because we definitely need a better plug for the work," Mel said.

"Oh yeah, my man from the East side said he got a new plug that wants to meet you. His name is Haitian John. Said he got it and his numbers are good," Cheese informed YC.

"I need to holla at him ASAP!" YC shouted.

Cheese got on his phone. "This is Cheese, my people said you want to meet up."

Haitian John smiled. "I can pull up on you now with some shit."

Cheese pressed the mute button on his phone. "He said he can pull up now with something," Cheese repeated to YC.

YC thought before responding. "Tell him to bring me a brick if he really about that life."

Cheese unmuted his phone. "Can you bring me a brick?"

"I'll do you one even better, I'll bring you one and match it with one on consignment," Haitian John proposed.

"He said he'll sell us one and front us one, what you think?" Cheese checked with YC before accepting the deal.

YC nodded his head in agreement. "Tell him let's do it."

"That's a bet, I'll text you the address," Cheese said.

"I'll be there within the hour," Haitian John responded before hanging up.

An hour later Haitian John pulled up to the bando in an all-white Maserati Quattroporte Modena playing one of YC's songs. He was blasting it loud enough that it got the attention of everyone in the bando. He let the music play for a minute before turning off the engine and exiting the vehicle.

He had a LV backpack as he approached the bando. "Come around to the back," Cheese commanded.

Haitian John walked around to the back and was let in by a young, slim soldier named Bee-stack. "Come this way," he said as he led Haitian John to the area where the gang hung out.

When Haitian John saw YC he knew exactly who he was, but he had to play it off as if he never laid eyes on him. YC stared at him with a peculiar expression, he always did this when he first met a man he was doing business with.

"Always look a man in his eye. If he can't hold your stare, he's hiding something," Jaybird had said to young YC.

YC just stared at Haitian John while Cheese handled the

business. "You said one brick was only $20K, that's $15K better than anyone in the tri-state area. I haven't seen numbers like this since 2015!" Cheese announced.

"You won't see these numbers anywhere. We got the best work for the best price. Hands down!" Haitian John bragged.

Cheese handed him $20K. "Here's the money for one brick."

Haitian John opened up the LV backpack and pulled out two bricks of pure cocaine. "Here you go. Two kilos of the best coke on the market."

Cheese took the bricks and stashed them. YC was still looking at Haitian John like he was living up to his moniker. Haitian John felt the energy. He didn't want to mess up the operation by being scared. He was uncomfortable with the way YC was staring at him.

"What was that music you were playing when you pulled up?" YC asked when Cheese went to stash the work.

"That's this cat my man G-Mack put me on to. He said he's been trying to connect with him. I was just playing it on the way over." Haitian John didn't want to trip any wires, but this was stretching it.

"Are you talking about G-Mack from Get Money Records?" YC asked.

"Yeah, you know him?"

"I know of him. I'm the nigga on the record you were listening to." YC stuck his hand out. "YC, nice to meet you homie."

Haitian John shook his hand. "You're YC! That's crazy, I was just with G-Mack yesterday. He texted me the link to your YouTube channel and I've been vibing to it! You're a talented brother. Let me call G." He pulled out his phone and called G-Mack, who picked up on the second ring. "What up G-Mack? Remember that cat YC you were looking for? I'm standing in front of him right now."

"Stop playing! Put me on speaker phone," G-Mack asked,

and his voice could be heard by everyone in the room. "YC! Brother I've been looking for you! If you can come to my office I have a super deal for you."

YC couldn't believe what was happening. "Where is your office? I'll be there in an hour tops!" YC was excited.

"John will give it to you. I look forward to meeting you." G-Mack hung up the phone.

Cheese and everyone in the room heard G-Mack. They all knew who he was because of the huge success of his flagship artist, Dirty Lo. YC was a fan of Dirty Lo's, he imagined doing songs with him. YC was shocked that all this was happening to him.

"You just said if you get a check you were going to do this rap shit for real. It looks like you're going to get that check, so what's up?" Cheese grabbed YC in a bear hug.

"You know what's up! I'm about to take the rap game over, my nigga!" YC said with confidence.

"If you want, you can follow me to G-Mack's office," Haitian John offered.

"That'll work," Cheese replied.

"Me and Cheese are going to meet with G-Mack. I need you to hold the fort down until we come back," YC said to Mel.

"You know I got you, my nigga." Mel gave YC a handshake.

On the way to G-Mack's office, YC and Cheese talked about what they would do with a million. They were daydreaming about making it big in the rap game. They were both from the bottom of the barrel of society. Although they were making a lot of money, they also spent a lot of money, faster than they made it sometimes. They both had gambling addictions that were out of control, so it was hard to save money.

When they got to Get Money Records headquarters, G-Mack was standing in the parking lot smoking a Cuban cigar. "Welcome to Get Money Records, my home and hopefully yours." G-Mack gave YC and Cheese handshakes.

"Thank you, G-Mack, I appreciate it," YC said with humility.

"Come this way." G-Mack led them through a myriad of offices with pretty women working on the phones to a studio. "Dirty Lo is in there cooking up some shit. Maybe after we talk I can see if you two can do a collaboration."

"That'll be dope!" Cheese spoke for YC who was tongue-tied.

G-Mack took them to his plush office. "Have a seat." YC and Cheese sat down directly across from G-Mack. "First things first, I definitely want to sign you to a three-album recording contract. Second, I don't want to waste your time and I don't want you to waste mine. I have a contract for $1.5 million for your signing bonus."

Cheese looked at YC and they both were flabbergasted at the quickness of the deal. He literally went from selling drugs out of an abandoned house, to being offered $1.5 million for the first recording contract of his life. YC was at a loss for words, and G-Mack saw it.

"So, what are you going to do? An opportunity like this only comes once in a lifetime." G-Mack paused and stared YC directly in his eyes like he always did individuals.

YC stared at G-Mack without blinking before speaking. "I'm fucking with it! Where do I sign?"

G-Mack handed him a pen. "Put your name, address, and your date of birth right here. Then you're going to sign right here, and you're all done."

YC didn't even read the contract before signing it. "Here you go." He handed G-Mack the contract.

"Welcome to the Get Money Records family!" G-Mack shook YC's hand. "Here is your check for $1.5 million. Congratulations!"

YC looked at the check as if it were a Martian with six heads. "Damn, that's a lot of zeros!"

"We on my nigga!" Cheese shouted.

"Let's get back to the trap, we left two bricks in there," YC reminded Cheese.

"Facts!" Cheese replied.

"Go straight to the bank to deposit that check, you don't want to lose it," G-Mack suggested.

"Damn, I don't have a bank. What can I do?" YC asked.

"Don't worry, I got you. I'll have my assistant start you a bank account tomorrow," G-Mack offered.

"Good looking, OG, I appreciate everything. I won't let you down." With that being said, Cheese and YC exited the building headed back to the bando.

When they were gone, Haitian John made the call to Agent Heron. "Two parts of the operation are done. I made contact and connected him with G-Mack," Haitian John reported.

"What happened when he met with G-Mack?" Agent Heron asked.

"He signed on the dotted line, just like we predicted," G-Mack added.

"That's good news! Damn, you guys work faster than my well-trained operatives. You might have a career in the intelligence community," Agent Heron said.

"I don't know about that, but lets' just say we get the job done," Haitian John responded.

"Okay, off to phase three of this operation. That's where we create the beef between Dirty Lo and Dirty Redd and throw YC in the mix," Agent Heron instructed.

"This part is going to be fun, because I can't stand Jay-Roc and his Billigoats!" G-Mack said with vengeance.

"You'll get your chance. For now, focus on getting YC famous. I'll work my magic on my end with YC." Agent Heron paused. "As for you, Haitian John, I need you to keep supplying them with the drugs. Double up on them even when they still got some. We have to move this coke, I have plenty to get rid of."

"I got you, let me work my magic," Haitian John mimicked Agent Heron's message.

"Yeah you do that." Agent Heron hung up and moved the pawn on the chessboard. "Something about Haitian John eats at me. Maybe it's because I know he's really a rat bastard that got saved by the agency." He moved his knight on the chessboard. He was playing chess with Director Cohen while talking on the phone.

"He's expendable. Once he made the contact, we can set up another guy to supply YC and his gang." Director Cohen moved his queen.

"Since our departure from Afghanistan, our heroin supply has dwindled. That's why the cocaine connection in South America has to resume until we can get another international heroin supplier," Agent Heron reported.

"We're working on finding the new heroin rich country we can exploit. We're looking at Columbia. The soil and climate are good enough to grow the poppy plant for heroin production," Director Cohen announced.

"Check," Agent Heron said while Director Cohen thought of a way out of check.

"Good move, Agent Heron." Director Cohen moved out of check.

Agent Heron took Cohen's queen. "You left your queen open."

Director Cohen smiled. "I knew you would see it that way." He moved his bishop. "Check mate!"

Agent Heron was stunned. "I must admit, I didn't see that coming." He shook Director Cohen's hand. "Nice move, Director."

"Make sure you have a tight leash on this new asset. Keep him in check. You lost control of Darius Jensen, we could lose everything if he pops up alive. We don't need any more glitches, understood?" Cohen gave Agent Heron a cold stare.

"Understood." Agent Heron nodded his head in agreement.

"I'll see you Friday after my meeting at the World Summit of Intelligence Agencies. I'm giving a speech on the future of the Intelligence Agency." Director Cohen exited Agent Heron's office.

Any word that D-Boy was alive would mean Agent Heron's immediate termination, literally. Director Cohen would also have some explaining to do. The agency had a strict policy for operatives that go rogue: death. It would be reported as an unfortunate accident, or some rare health issue.

Agent Heron was running a rogue operation with Agent Sparrow off the books. That's why Sparrow was at her own mercy because the resources of the agency weren't funding this operation. This was Director Cohen and Agent Heron's secret band-aid operation to fix the mistakes they made with D-Boy.

John and D-Boy had enough evidence to take down the entire agency. They had proof of direct contact with an agent of a major American Intelligence Agency as the kingpin of a multi-million-dollar drug business. John compiled enough evidence before they faked their deaths to send Director Cohen and Agent Heron to jail for life and dismantle the agency for good.

Agent Heron poured a double shot of the bourbon and drank it down, then poured another. The pressure of this rogue operation was taking a toll on him. It wouldn't take much time for an investigator to figure out Sparrow was an agent and link her directly to Agent Heron.

Agent Heron sipped on his second round. "That fucking D-Boy!" he shouted to himself in anger before finishing the double shot in one gulp.

THE WORLD SUMMIT **OF INTELLIGENCE AGENCIES, DAVOS, SWITZERLAND**

The lavish conference room accommodated the wealthiest tycoons on the planet. Owners of multi-national corporations, heads of state, banking industries, and media conglomerates were all in attendance. They waited for the man of the hour, the key-speaker, to give his speech on the future of the intelligence community.

"Ladies and distinguished gentleman, I'm proud to be here with you at the thirtieth annual World Summit of Intelligence Agencies," said the well-known computer giant Gill Bates. "We have a lot of innovative ideas for the future of the technology of intelligence agencies across the globe. This next speaker needs no introduction, he is the Michael Jordan of spies, the Director of the Central Intelligence Agency, Mr. Antonio Cohen." Gill shook Director Cohen's hand before walking away from the podium.

"Good evening. It is a great time to be alive! We are on the precipice of a new day for the Intelligence Agency. No longer will we play the background, waiting to take our orders from weak, incompetent leaders. We will create our position secretly, covertly like we always have in our past. Only this time we will influence elections and policies, we will put our people in leadership positions. Once we have achieved our goal of placing an agent in every key role of power then we will claim the victory the founders always wanted. A world where all governments will answer to the intelligence community, not the other way around. That time is now!" Director Cohen shouted as the room burst into a standing ovation. "It's our time to live high on the hog. Why should we do all the dirty work and receive crumbs from the spoils of our efforts? If we all band together, and really do the work to achieve the goals I set forth, nothing can stop us. We will enjoy a reign the likes of the world's longest lasting empires. Are you with me? I said are you with me?" The entire crowd exploded in cheer again for Director Cohen's speech.

Director Cohen smiled with thoughts of ultimate power running through his mind.

Gill Bates was impressed with Director Cohen's speech, so much so that he wanted to speak to him about an offer. Gill was in the tech business, but he wanted in on the drug business and he knew the CIA were the real top players.

"Excuse me, Director Cohen, but may I have a word with you in private?" Gill motioned for him to get in the limousine so they could have privacy.

Director Cohen obliged and got in. "What can I do for you, Mr. Bates?"

"I'm going to be short and to the point. I want in on the drug business. For a 10 percent stake I'm willing to cut you in on 5 percent of my new venture with vaccines," Gill proposed.

"Why would I give up 10 percent for 5 percent?" Cohen asked.

"Because at 1 percent it's valued at over $100 million. At 5 percent that's over $500 million guaranteed. You can't give me the same guarantee on my money because the drug business is illegal and can be subject to search, seizures and all that kind of mess," Gill explained.

"What's my guarantee that your vaccines won't pan out to be useless? There's no emergency to warrant massive vaccinations," Cohen responded.

"Oh, that's where you're wrong. I'll let you in on a little secret, next year there will be another pandemic. This one will be even more strict than the first one. We're putting the vaccine in the food for those that refuse to take the shot. So you see Director Cohen, the future of vaccines is written in stone." Gill gave Cohen a devilish grin.

"In that case you can count me in." Cohen shook Gill's hand to seal the deal.

Gill poured two glasses of Clicquot from the mini bar. "Here's to an uncertain future for the masses, but a fortunate one for us." They clicked their glasses together in celebration.

CHAPTER 11
ASTORIA QUEENS, NEW YORK

D-Boy and John purchased luxury apartments right next door to each other in a posh section of Astoria Queens. It was low-key and upscale. It had that 'in the cut' appearance that they were looking for. They were back in the states, which was one of the goals, the other plan was to clear their names.

John had a plan to exonerate them from any persecution. He gathered intel on Agent Heron, enough to prove the intent to distribute drugs on behalf of the United States government. John knew he was up against some dangerous people, but he had to clear D-Boy and himself from the tentacles of the agency.

D-Boy was just happy to be back in the states. Dubai was cool, but after seven years he craved the smell of the New York City streets. D-Boy was back in his element, the gritty streets of New York. In the seven years he had been gone he imagined how much it changed, but to his surprise it was the same way he left it.

"Listen, I know you want to go buy a luxury car and wear expensive clothes and jewelry, but now isn't the time. We don't need to draw any unnecessary attention to ourselves," John said to D-Boy.

"Come on man! I waited seven years to come back and now I

103

can't even spend my money on things that I like," D-Boy protested.

"I want to live my normal life, too, but I don't want to be arrested for Death Fraud either. We have to absolve ourselves first, because the agency will not stop if they know we're alive. So, I'm going to bring it to them before they have a chance to react," John said like an expert.

"Okay, but how long is your plan going to take before we can get back to being Americans?"

"It may take up to seven years, hopefully less. At any rate we're not in any position to parade around like a target."

"At least tell me your plan!"

"I've compiled enough evidence to exonerate us. The only problem is getting the info to the right person that isn't compromised by the agency," John explained.

"I get it, we can think someone is on our side, but they might still be the ops," D-Boy said in street language.

"What are the ops?"

"Oh, the word ops is short for the opposition or the other side."

"Okay, well our 'ops' are very powerful and dangerous. So, we have to be extra careful how we move."

"I get it, we have to stay on the down low."

"When I receive our new identities we can ditch the Arab masks and just rock our regular faces."

"I can't wait to take this stupid mask off."

"Me either. I was starting to lose myself."

"Me, too. Especially when I have to talk with the accent."

"Well, it won't be too long before we can stop the Arab act once and for all. Until then, we're both from Dubai here on a work Visa."

"Whatever, today I'm going to hang out with my nephew and my brother. I'll see you later."

"Just be careful if you run into Dirty Redd's girl, Sarah. I'm still not too sure about her," John warned.

"I got you, John," D-Boy said before exiting John's apartment headed for his brother's mansion.

LONG ISLAND, NEW YORK, DIRTY REDD'S HOUSE

Dirty Redd was originally from Queens, New York, but he bought his house on Long Island. He always said if he ever got rich he would live on Long Island. Well, Dirty Redd was worth $12.7 million, so he did what he always dreamed of. His house was a mini-mansion, way more than he needed as a single man with no kids.

Since they returned to the states, Sarah had a serious attitude with Dirty Redd. She was confrontational and argumentative everyday over little things. "Do you have to chew so loud? It's so annoying!" She abruptly removed herself from the dinner table and went to the bathroom.

"What's your problem? I can't even chew my food without it being an issue!" He got up, grabbed the keys to his Bentley and departed from the house.

When he was gone, Sarah took that opportunity to check in with Agent Heron. "I can't take this shit!" Sarah shouted when Agent Heron answered.

"Calm down, what seems to be the problem?" Agent Heron had to ease her mind because he needed her at her best. "If I were to send you $100K would that make you feel any better? I need you at your best to finish the mission."

"Yeah, you can definitely send me $100K. But most of all I just want to finish the mission so I can get on to the next mission. This guy is so annoying I can't take him anymore. I don't like him for real, and it's taking a toll on me."

"Check your bank account. I just sent you the money."

Sarah looked at her account and the money just landed. "Yeah I got the money, thank you Agent Heron. I'm going to finish the job." She took a deep breath.

"That-a-girl! Just a few more weeks tops and it'll all be over. Then me and you can take a month vacation anywhere on the planet."

"I'm definitely going to take you up on your proposal when this is said and done."

"As for now, stay on the Arab guys. Their identities checked out as emissaries of the United Arab Emirates, but if you have a hunch go with your instincts. I have to go now, I'll speak to you in one week." Agent Heron hung up the phone.

Sarah was so agitated that she decided to take a long walk. She didn't understand why she was so aggravated lately. She couldn't put her finger on it, but something was going on with her biologically. She knew herself, and this wasn't her. She kept blaming it on Dirty Redd, but there was something else at play, because he wasn't really the problem.

She walked on the sidewalk and observed the nice houses in the area. You could tell this neighborhood was upper-class. Dirty Redd's house was mediocre compared to the other houses in the neighborhood. She kept walking, then she suddenly got nauseous and threw up on someone's freshly cut grass.

"What the fuck is wrong with me?" she asked herself. "It can't be what I'm thinking it is, no way," she said to herself as she tried to do the math. "My period is freaking late!"

She took an Uber to the local supermarket. She was there for one thing, so she went straight to the women's section and bought herself a paternity test. She took another Uber back to Dirty Redd's house and went straight to the bathroom to urinate on the pregnancy test stick. It didn't take five minutes before the test came back positive.

"No fucking way!" she shouted. She took another test, and it came back positive, too. "FUCK ME!" *This explains my attitude. I knew something was wrong because I'm never this bitchy.*

Sarah had an IUD birth control device implanted. Apparently, she was still pregnant despite the IUD implant. All that sex she was having with Dirty Redd broke down the barrier and his sperm still impregnated her. It was rare, but things like this did happen.

"What the fuck am I going to do now? I don't want to have this man's baby, but I don't believe in abortion either. What the fuck am I doing?" Sarah spoke to herself in the mirror as if her reflection was going to answer her question.

As she contemplated her dilemma, the front door flung open. "Baby! I have something for you." It was Dirty Redd, he had a large bouquet of red roses and a box of chocolates.

She came to the front to see Dirty Redd smiling. "What's this?" she asked, surprised.

"I just wanted you to know I understand what you're going through. I wanted to make your pregnancy as easy as possible." He smiled and handed her the roses and the box of chocolates.

Although Sarah was a hardened killer for the agency, she still had that female streak. "Dirty, you didn't have to do this." She felt the lump in her throat and her eyes were already welling up for the tears to start.

Dirty Redd saw Sarah getting emotional, so he hugged her. "It's okay, I'm here for you and the baby. I'm never letting you and my baby go, I'll always be here," Dirty Redd declared.

Sarah couldn't stop the tears from flowing down her cheeks. "You're such a good man, I don't deserve you, I really don't."

"Why are you saying that? You deserve me and so much more." Dirty Redd was confused because he thought she'd be happy.

"It's not you, it's me. I have issues that I need to resolve. Please let me deal with my demons." Sarah ran to the bedroom and shut the door.

Dirty Redd took that as a sign to give her some space, so he just left the house and went for a drive. He needed to talk to someone about his situation with Sarah. Even though she made him promise not to tell anyone about her pregnancy, he needed to vent. What better person for Dirty Redd to consult with than Mouf? He knew Dirty Redd too well, and Mouf was known to give out the best advice.

"I'm about to pull up on you. I need to talk to you about something important," Dirty Redd said on the phone.

"How do you know I'm not busy with a woman or something? You always think I'm available for you like I'm on call," Mouf protested.

"I'm in the driveway, open the door," Dirty Redd demanded.

"Damn nigga! You could've given me more heads up before you just pop up, but alright." Mouf came to the door in his beloved Versace robe. "I'm going to start charging people for my advice."

Dirty Redd entered. "Bro' this is some serious shit I have to tell you." He took a deep breath.

"Spit it out," Mouf said playfully.

"I wasn't supposed to tell anyone but—"

"Sarah is prego," Mouf cut Dirty Redd off mid-sentence.

"How the fuck did you know?" Dirty Redd asked, confused.

"It doesn't take a rocket scientist to figure out the woman was trying to get pregnant from day one." Mouf raised his eyebrows and smirked at the same time. "Second, I know you. You fall in love so easy. I bet you don't know her momma's name," Mouf said sarcastically.

"You're a fucking psychic! You always put some shit together. That's my issue, she's becoming difficult for me to deal with. I can't even buy her roses and chocolate to make her feel better. I don't know what else to do."

"You know what your main problem is, Dirty? You move too loose to be a celebrity. We're rap stars, we can have as many women as we please. Some men feast while others starve, I'm feasting, you out here acting like a thirst bucket falling for any bitch that breathes on you!" Mouf shook his head in disgust.

"You right about some shit but come on, thirst bucket? I'll admit it, I fell in love quick, but shorty was acting different when I met her in Dubai. Now she's acting like she hates my guts," Dirty Redd spoke in a sentimental tone.

"I get it, but the definition of insanity is doing the same thing and expecting different results. Brother, stop the insanity! If you'll excuse me, I have twins in my room waiting for me to return. We'll talk more about this later." Mouf opened the front door and motioned for Dirty Redd to exit.

"Oh, I didn't know you had company. You could've told me I would've called—" Dirty Redd stopped himself, closed his eyes and held his head low before continuing. "I was getting ready to say I'll just call Prime. I still can't believe he's gone," Dirty Redd said with sorrow.

"Me either. I was about to call him yesterday until I realized he's gone. That reminds me, do you want to add another third member? Or we'll just be a duo," Mouf asked.

"I hadn't thought about that." Dirty Redd paused to think about the situation. "No one can replace Prime! We'll just be a duo, besides no one is worthy to pick up where Prime left off."

"Then it's settled, we are officially a duo!" Mouf declared as they shook hands to seal the deal.

"I'll catch you later, don't hurt yourself in there with those two." Dirty Redd exited the house and drove off headed back home.

Mouf walked into the room and two beautiful Latin identical twins sat up and spoke in unison, "We missed you, Daddy."

Mouf untied his Versace robe. "I missed you, too." He let his robe drop to the floor and he shut the bedroom door.

———

GET MONEY STUDIOS, **EAST ATLANTA, GA**

YC and Cheese were standing in front of the entrance of Get Money Studios waiting to be buzzed in. G-Mack opened the door. "Come in fellas." YC and Cheese came through the door and G-Mack led them to studio A where Dirty Lo was recording.

YC and Cheese were starstruck as they watched Dirty Lo through the plexiglass while he recorded new material. This was YC's dream come true, to be in the studio with Dirty Lo. YC just started rapping a year ago and started taking it seriously three months ago. Now he has signed a $1.5 million recording contract with the biggest label in Atlanta. And he was recording a song with his favorite artist of all time, Dirty Lo.

Dirty Lo took the headphones off, exited the booth and entered the control room. The first thing he did was greet YC. "You must be YC, nice to meet you bro'." Dirty Lo gave YC and Cheese handshakes.

"This my partner, Cheese. It's nice to meet you brother, I'm a huge fan of your music," YC said humbly.

"Naw dog, I'm a fan of your shit! G-Mack played some of your music for me and I was blown away at the way you deliver your bars. So surreal." Dirty Lo complimenting YC gave him confidence as a new artist.

"I appreciate you, big bro', for real that means a lot to me."

"Don't mention it. Hey, you want to jump on this diss record I'm doing about that fake nigga Dirty Redd from the Billigoats?" Dirty Lo asked.

"Man, fuck that nigga, I never like them New York niggas anyway. They think niggas from the South is slow or something. We're getting just as much money or more than them niggas from New York!" YC declared.

"That's what the fuck I'm talking about!" Dirty Lo gave YC another handshake solidifying their union against Dirty Redd.

The first day they banged out three songs back-to-back disrespecting Dirty Redd, Billigoats, and the whole American D-Boy

Records. They didn't stop there, the next day they shot three music videos for all three songs and put them out immediately. To add insult to injury, in one of the songs called "Lil' Dirty Boy," Dirty Lo dissed Prime knowing he was killed in Dubai. They were even on social media going live talking trash about Dirty Redd.

The live social media rant quickly caught the attention of Dirty Redd. "Yo, you hear this dude Dirty Lo going the fuck off on me?" Dirty Redd asked Mouf.

"Yeah, that shit is all over the internet. You already know, I'll meet you in the studio in an hour," Mouf said calmly. He was the quiet riot.

"Say less." Dirty Redd grabbed his old school marble note-book he wrote songs in, and a pen. He exited his house headed for American D-Boy studios in mid-town Manhattan. "Oh it's on boy!" Dirty Redd said as he sped on the Long Island Expressway.

CHAPTER 12
DOWNTOWN ATLANTA, GA, GREYHOUND BUS TERMINAL

Fernando and Diego got off the Greyhound bus in downtown Atlanta. When they stepped inside the terminal they saw a bunch of homeless people and drug addicts. Some of the worst of Atlanta's undesirables end up at the Greyhound bus terminal. This is where they come to beg and steal, or to use drugs and go to sleep. It is a rest haven for bums.

It was a culture shock for Fernando and Diego. They were under the impression that all Americans were living the life of luxury. This was a rude awakening for them. The smell of human urine and bad hygiene filled the air like a blanket of funk. Vagabonds of all colors congregating, waiting for unsuspecting newcomers to victimize. Fernando and Diego fit the description perfectly.

"Excuse me but can I get some money to buy something to eat?" a dirty woman that smelled terrible asked Diego.

While their attention was averted a short, bald, Black man crept up and grabbed Fernando's suitcase and ran. "Hey!" Fernando shouted as he began to chase the man, he was tripped by another bum.

The bum that tripped him laughed. "That's what you get, stupid!"

"Chase him! I'll stay here with your luggage," Fernando ordered.

Diego chased the two bums as they ran through the back blocks. When they reached a remote alley where there were no onlookers, both men waited for Diego to get closer. "Come on, amigo, let's see what you got," one of the bums said while revealing his knife. "I'll make a taco out of you!"

Diego stood calmly. "I don't want to hurt you, just give me the luggage."

"Oh, you're going to hurt me, I think it's going to be the other way around, amigo." He lunged forward with the knife.

Before the bum could take another step, Diego pulled out his weapon and fired it at the man's chest. He fell to the ground and the other guy took off running. Diego picked up the suitcase and calmly walked back to the terminal where Fernando was waiting. They didn't want to bring any attention to themselves.

Fernando saw a taxi. "Excuse me, can you take us to this address?"

"Sure, that's on the southside," the cabdriver replied.

Fernando and Diego placed their luggage in the trunk and got in the back seat. On the way there they both remained quiet and marveled at the urban scenery. They had heard about America from folklore, but the real thing was aesthetically depressing. For blocks all they saw was poor Black people living in poverty. Much like the neighborhoods that they came from, the only difference was that the people were Latin instead of Black.

When they arrived at their destination they were greeted by more confrontation. "Who the fuck are you?" the old Black woman named Milly said as they reached the doorstep. She was the landlord.

"I am Fernando, and this is my brother Diego. We are the new tenants," Fernando explained politely.

"Oh shit! I forgot about yawl. Come on in." She opened the door for them. "I'm Mildred but everybody calls me Milly."

"Nice to meet you, Milly," Diego said.

"Come this way, I'll show you to your apartment." She took them around to the side of the house where the entrance to their apartment was located and opened the door. "This is your new apartment."

They looked around at a disgusting living room. Then she took them to the bedroom areas that were just as bad as the living room. There was writing on the walls, the carpet smelled like mildew, and there was no air conditioning. Living in Atlanta with no air conditioning was like living in their country; the conditions were the same.

"I'll let you two settle in, here's the key. Your rent is paid up for six months, so you won't be seeing me a lot." She shuffled her feet out of the front door and closed it behind her.

"Damn! King Cobra promised us the best accommodations! This is worse than where we lived in Columbia," Diego was fuming.

"Don't worry my friend, if my plan works we will have a mansion in six months," Fernando said confidently.

"What is this plan?" Diego asked.

"We're going to become our own boss. We're going to find some dealers and we're going to supply them. That's how we're going to get rich in America." Fernando was enthusiastic about his aspirations.

"How are we going to get the drugs?" Diego asked.

Fernando smiled. "Before we left I told my plan to my little brother Ricardo. He's going to organize the transportation of 100 kilos directly to us once I tell him my location."

"You sneaky bastard! You've been planning this for months and you didn't say a word." Diego was impressed.

"I knew if the word got out that we were growing our own coke Cobra would kill us slow. We all heard what he did to Carlos." King Cobra boiled him alive.

"Yeah I remember, that's why you're crazy for doing this. I'm with you regardless." Diego gave Fernando a handshake.

"Now that I know where I'll be, I'm going to text Ricardo my address and the drugs will be here in a week," Fernando confirmed by sending Ricardo their address. "Done! Now all we have to do is get some good customers, ones that buy kilos, and in no time we'll both be millionaires."

They unpacked with thoughts of becoming rich. America was the land of opportunity for men like Fernando and Diego. They both knew what it meant to starve or to be barefoot because you can't afford shoes. They would talk often about making it big, that's why they joined the Lost Souls. It was a way up for young men in Cali Columbia.

King Cobra was known to take young men from the slums and fill their heads up with dreams. He would pay people to recruit and promote propaganda that he pays the most and treats his soldiers the best out of any cartel. After a year of spreading his campaign, he had amassed an army the size of the Columbian National Guard. That's how the Lost Souls Cartel became the largest and most feared drug cartel in Columbia.

The truth was that King Cobra was merciless to his soldiers. He killed them sometimes for sport. If they did anything he didn't permit he would torture them. Some soldiers had to rob and steal because they didn't get paid in a month. King Cobra didn't pay what he owed, if you asked he would punish you for calling him a liar.

"So you're saying that I didn't pay you for a month. I'm Saying that every man in my organization gets paid every month," King Cobra said.

"I didn't receive any pay for the whole month of April," one of his soldiers responded.

King Cobra backhanded him so hard his nose bled. "You are calling me a liar!" he yelled.

"No sir." The man took his lick and stumbled away.

It was examples like that, that made Fernando want out of Lost Souls. He hated the name Lost Souls. Fernando and Diego were spiritual, so they didn't agree that their souls were lost. In fact, they were both believed to be men of God in their communities. They joined to escape poverty, not because they agreed that their souls were lost.

"Get some rest, we have a lot to do for the Lost Souls. Not for long," Fernando said.

"Good night brother," Diego replied.

They both pretended to be sleep, thoughts of being rich kept them up thinking about their future.

―――――

LENOX SQUARE MALL, BUCKHEAD, ATLANTA

YC and Cheese were running up the bag of money YC just got. It took a week for his check to clear because he had to start a bank account to begin with. YC was hood for real, he didn't believe in credit, so he bought everything cash. He never had a bank account. If he had a check he cashed it at Walmart.

Now he had $1.5 million in his new bank account. Today he decided to spend about $50K on designer clothes for himself and his capo, Cheese. What better place to buy all the latest high-end designer clothes than the notorious Lenox Mall? They grew up wanting to come here and spend thousands on clothes and not caring about it. Today was that day for them.

"I can't believe it man!" Cheese said as he tried on a $2,500 Gucci sweat suit.

"Believe it. You're the one that told me I could do it, and I did it!" YC was as excited as a kid on the first day of school.

"I know, it just seems like a dream and I'm just watching you do it." Cheese was YC's only real friend.

"They tried to give me some janky ass nigga as a manager. I told them you were going to be my manager. You might as well, you know how to handle me better than some stranger." YC put Cheese on notice of his new position.

"You already know! I got you my nigga, to the moon and back!" Cheese was smiling from ear to ear.

"Excuse me but are you YC?" a beautiful redbone girl asked.

"Why yes I am. And who are you besides gorgeous?" YC was smooth with the ladies.

She smiled perfect rows of white teeth. "My name is Makeda, take my number. What're you doing later?" she asked shyly.

"I got a show with Dirty Lo at the Tabernacle, you should come through. I'll put you on the guest list," YC informed her.

"Definitely! I'll see you there, YC." She giggled before she walked away.

"Damn!" YC said when he saw her bodacious butt. "Did you see her ass, bro'?"

"You know she got friends. All the baddies run in packs," Cheese replied.

"That's a fact!" They were at the cash register with arms full of clothes and Gucci belts.

The cashier quickly rang up their items. "That'll be $16,473.89." She waited for his reaction to the total.

"That's it?" YC pulled out a wad of cash from one pocket. "Throw in that Gucci bucket hat!"

She grabbed it and added up the new total. "The new total is $17,013.24."

YC counted the money a thousand at a time. "Here's $16,900." He added two more-hundred-dollar bills. "You can keep the change." Another girl assisted the cashier with bagging all the clothes up in signature Gucci shopping bags.

They walked out of Gucci looking like brand-new money. People were starting to notice YC from the three music videos he made with Dirty Lo. He saw them looking, usually he would ask, *what the fuck you looking at?* He knew why they were looking, and he welcomed the attention.

"Excuse me, I don't mean to bother you, but are you YC?" a teenage boy asked.

"Yeah that's me, how are you doing brother?" YC shook the young man's hand.

"You killed that verse on that song "Closed Casket!" I fast-forward it to your part every time I listen to it." The teen boy was starstruck. "Can you take this pic with me so I can post it on Instagram?"

"Sure, Cheese can you take the picture for us?" YC asked.

Cheese grabbed his phone and snapped the pic. "Here you go buddy." He handed his phone back.

"Thank you! I'm going to school tomorrow to show every-body!" He walked off happy.

"That was crazy!" Cheese said.

"I know, I have to get used to it. It's better than getting looks because of beef. I can deal with this all day!" YC responded.

"Speaking of looks because of beef." Cheese nodded to the three guys wearing red bandannas staring at him and YC. "That's them Blood niggas from Old National we were beefing with."

"I remember them niggas. You got the blickey on you?" YC asked feeling the energy.

"It's in the car," Cheese answered.

"Fuck! We have to get to it. These fools want smoke. We going to give it to them!" YC picked up the pace, Cheese followed suit.

When they looked back the three bloods were following them to the parking lot. YC picked up the pace, the car was only twenty feet away. When he looked back he saw one of them reach under his shirt. The next few seconds moved in slow motion as YC sprinted desperately to the car to reach the weapon. Cheese was a few feet behind YC when YC opened the door to the car.

POP! POP! POP! POP!

The gunfire went off in rapid succession, hitting the car door and the front windshield.

YC was able to grab the gun and let off four of his own shots. BOOM! BOOM! BOOM! BOOM!

"Hold that!" He saw one of the blood's shoulders jerk back from catching the bullet. They ran the other way to their vehicle.

"I hit one of them niggas!"

Waiting for a response from Cheese, YC turned his head, looking around for him.

"Cheese!"

He walked to the other side of the car and saw Cheese lying on the ground in a pool of his own blood. Two of the bullets hit Cheese, one in the back of the head and one in the back. The bullet to the back hit his spine, so even if he survived he would have been a paraplegic. But with the bullet to the back of the head, Cheese was dead.

"Fuck! Damn, Cheese!" YC's eyes welled up with tears that flooded his face. "Why? You were about to be right there with me, at the top."

Lenox Mall was always heavily guarded because of past incidents like this. The Atlanta Police Department was there within minutes. "Requesting an ambulance. Victim is a young Black man, he is deceased."

They took YC down for questioning and let him go after determining he was an innocent bystander. The news caught on quick, they were waiting with lights and cameras when YC exited the precinct. They were shoving microphones in his face. There were six networks waiting to get a word from YC.

"Do you know who shot your friend?" a Fox Atlanta reporter asked.

"Was it gang related?" another reporter from the Shade Room asked.

"I don't know anything. All I know is I lost my best friend.

Please leave me alone before I bug the fuck out!" YC made his way through the sea of reporters, ignoring their questions.

A Maybach truck pulled up. "Get in!" It was G-Mack, so YC obliged. "What the fuck happened? You can be straight with me," G-Mack assured.

"It was some old beef with some Blood niggas from Old National," YC was straightforward with G-Mack.

"So, you know who it was which is good. They'll be taken care of within twenty-four hours," G-Mack said matter-of-factly.

"I got this. I take care of my own beef," YC replied.

"Okay, have it your way. But for now, I need you to lay low," G-Mack ordered.

"I got you. Just take me to my condo. I just want to be alone."

G-Mack dropped YC off at his new condo in Buckhead. It was fifteen minutes from the Lenox Mall where he just witnessed his best friend get killed. He looked around at the plush condo with all its luxury and felt empty. Without Cheese this wasn't going to be the experience YC expected. He wanted to live life to the fullest with the one person that really believed in him from the start.

"Bro' not only are you spitting that gangster shit, but you're also living it! These rap niggas are not living nothing they rap about! You the realest nigga that's coming out of Atlanta!" YC reminisced on all the times Cheese would encourage him to be a rapper.

"I'm not going to let you down." YC sparked the huge blunt he had sitting in the ashtray and took an enormous pull. He choked when he exhaled. He smoked until he was super-high, then his phone went off. "Hello, who this?"

"It's Makeda, you met me at Lenox today. You okay? I heard what happened today, it's all over the news. I was just calling to see if you wanted someone to comfort you in your time of need," Makeda said in a seductive tone.

"Yeah, that would be nice. I could use a female's comfort right now, especially a beautiful one at that," YC replied.

"Thank you, that was nice for you to say. Send me your address, I'll be there as soon as possible," Makeda said before hanging up the phone.

YC thought about Makeda. *Shorty is bad as fuck.*

It didn't take no time before his Ring camera doorbell went off. He looked at his phone and saw Makeda wearing high heels and a trench coat. She looked so sexy that YC's nature began to rise. He cracked his neck and his fingers and looked in the mirror to see himself before answering the door.

"Hello." She opened her trench coat to reveal a sexy maid's uniform. "Did you order maid service?" She showed the most seductive smile YC ever saw from a woman.

"Yes I did!" He led her in and closed the door.

CHAPTER 13
AMERICAN D-BOY RECORDS HEADQUARTERS

The entire staff was required to show up to this mandatory meeting at the American D-Boy Records office. Jay-Roc had a lot of concerns he wanted to address with the whole staff. Something was happening, the fans weren't gravitating to the Billigoats new diss music toward Dirty Lo and YC onslaught.

"We are getting slaughtered on the airwaves!" Jay-Roc shouted. "This new cat YC has made a name for himself by dissing our whole record label. The radio stations, for some reason, only play their songs. When it comes to playing the Billigoats response records, the DJs are ghosting us."

"I've been sending that new record to the same DJ pool that we've used for seven years," stated Darrell, the head of marketing. "I've been beefing with them every day about them not honoring our agreement."

"What is the response?" Jay-Roc asked.

"That it's politics, I keep saying what politics because this never happened before. When I send out singles they get played ASAP!" Darrell explained.

"All you hear on the radio is the three diss records from Dirty Lo and YC. Then to add insult to injury, immediately after the murder of YC's best friend Cheese the records tripled in streams." Sheila was a member of the marketing team.

"I'm telling you, Jay, it's like the DJ's and the radio are boycotting us or something," Mouf said. "Even the DJ's that really fuck with us aren't spinning us in the clubs in rotation. We are losing our steam!" Mouf declared.

"It's because they're in the South, they have a bigger market than we do," Dirty Redd said. "That's where they're killing us and the fact that it seems like DJ's are turning their backs on us all of a sudden."

"If we have to increase the budget for marketing to pay out more than I'm willing to do that. I'll be damned if I just let the ship sink without trying to save it," Jay-Roc spoke like the coach of a defeated team.

"We still got two new singles that haven't dropped that might be the saving grace of the label," Mouf added.

"Well, we need to do something, we're getting pummeled! If we don't do it now, we might not have a label," Jay-Roc spoke with a serious tone. No one spoke after him. "Let's get out there and push these new records to the limit!"

Everyone disbursed from the meeting with mixed feelings. Half of the staff felt they had a fighting chance to revive the label. The other half wanted to jump ship before it fully sank. Since its inception, American D-Boy has had nothing but success, this would be the first time it experienced hardship.

When everyone exited the conference room, Jay-Roc walked to his office, which was locked. He tapped three times and D-Boy opened the door. D-Boy wasn't in his Arab disguise anymore. All he had was dark shades and a New York Yankee ball cap pulled low.

"Not much of a disguise," Jay-Roc said when he saw his brother with no mask.

"Our new ID's came in so you can say goodbye to Mustafa. What's going on with the label?" D-Boy asked.

"We're bleeding. Our sales are down, radio play is dwindling, and the DJs aren't fucking with us. All because of some new cat from Atlanta named YC. Dirty Redd and Dirty Lo have been going back and forth for two years and it didn't impact us. Now he does three diss records with YC and the whole world has flipped on the entire American D-Boy empire!" Jay-Roc was furious.

D-Boy thought about everything Jay-Roc said and one thing came to mind. "This sounds like something John taught me called the Unseen Hand. Whenever an unseen turn of events occurs, the masses are trained to think the cause is natural, when in fact it was all designed by hands you never see." D-Boy paused to let it sink in.

"The mere fact that things happened all of a sudden is an indication that we're being sabotaged. I'm going to get John on this, he'll be able to figure it all out." D-Boy walked to the door and stopped before exiting. "Watch your back, I smell something fishy."

"*No*, you watch your back. Be careful, D-Boy," Jay-Roc said before D-Boy left the office.

D-Boy had a hunch who was behind this, none other than Special Agent Heron from the CIA. He didn't want to spook Jay-Roc with it, so he didn't mention him. Jay-Roc didn't need the extra headache of knowing that the CIA was back in their lives. It only meant more human suffering whenever they were involved. They destroy lives and move on as if nothing happened.

D-Boy was feeling guilty. He just came back into Jay-Roc's life and now things are falling apart. "If I would've stayed my ass away none of this shit would be happening." He took out his phone and called John. "We have a problem, I think Agent Heron is going after my brother and the label."

"That's funny, I was just about to call you. I have some good news concerning our situation. I'll bring you up to speed, meet me at our spot." John made D-Boy memorize catch phrases so no one would know if they were listening.

"Copy." D-Boy hung up the phone and headed toward Chelsea Piers, Downtown Manhattan.

When D-Boy arrived, John was already there. "We have to get you a better disguise, I recognized you a mile away." John was wearing a wig and round John Lennon glasses that made him look like a hippy.

"I thought you said we were good on the mask?" D-Boy asked.

"I said we were good on the mask, but we still have to wear a disguise, something light, like a beard or something to throw people off. You're walking around barefaced looking like the ghost of D-Boy. You were very popular in New York City, I wasn't. I'll get you a cool disguise that you can handle, I know you're tired of the mask." John got to know D-Boy well in the seven years they were on the run.

"What's your good news?" D-Boy asked curiously.

"I got a way to contact Senator Green from the Oversight Committee to expose Special Agent Heron and to finally exonerate us." John was hopeful they could pull it off.

"That's great news! When are you going to meet with him?" D-Boy was excited.

"That's the thing, my contact is undercover so we can't just speak with Senator Green directly without getting all the evidence to him first. It's a longshot but it's the only shot we have." John was a bit disappointed he couldn't just contact Senator Green without the red tape.

"At least we got something. What's going on with my brother and the label is what I want to tell you about." D-Boy paused. "It has Special Agent Heron written all over it." D-Boy explained what was going on at American D-Boy Records. "It's your Unseen Hand philosophy."

"You're right, my dear Watson," John made a humorous

reference to Sherlock Holmes, "You sound like you were listening to all those teachings I gave you in Dubai. The CIA have been involved with the music and film industry since the 1960s with Operation: MK ULTRA, where they used mind control techniques on celebrities. It was exposed and the CIA made claims about banning that operation, but we know they never did. The MK ULTRA operation just went deep underground and still operates 'til this day. They have their tentacles all over the music industry, from controlling radio to social media algorithms. They can definitely control the way the fans will receive a new artist, and they can make artist into stars overnight. We used to call it 'Micro-Wavy', because of the way they can make you wavy in minutes."

"I like that, Micro-Wavy. What you know about Wavy?" D-Boy was intrigued by John's knowledge of the word.

"My firm represented Max B, a.k.a. Wavy Crockett. From my understanding, he created the word. When I saw how creative he was I used the word and added Micro based on the truth that they can instantly make you popular," John explained.

"What's our next move?" D-Boy asked.

"It seems that this rapper, YC, is Agent Heron's new pawn to sell drugs for him. We need to make contact with YC and get him to understand what he's dealing with without blowing our cover. If we push him the wrong way it could backfire on him and us. Agent Heron will know we're alive, and YC will be murdered because he knows too much." John was very strategic in his thinking.

"I get what you're saying. If we are too direct he could sound the alarm before he agrees with some strangers. That will definitely get him killed if Heron discovers he knows he's been working for an agent of the CIA. That's what got us into the shit we're in."

"My sentiments exactly. That's why when we give YC the

info he understands he can't let them know he knows anything," John reflected on a plan.

"That's the hard part. How can we insure he won't run his mouth once we tell him?"

"It reminds me of a tactic we used in the MASAD. I call it a 'Reverse Honey Trap'." John smiled at the logic of his thinking.

"I know what a 'Honey Trap' is. That's where you use a beautiful woman to seduce a man and secretly take photos and video, then blackmail and bribe them for what you want. Explain a 'Reverse Honey Trap'," D-Boy spoke like a student with high honors.

"I'm impressed! You regurgitate information very well," John complemented D-Boy before continuing, "A 'Reverse Honey Trap' is where we lay everything on the table, then we use a woman he's already in love with and hold her life over his head if he decides to say anything. If we can get YC to switch sides and pledge allegiance to us, we can kill two birds with one stone. We can clear our names and put a stop to Agent Heron's drug operation, and we can end YC's destruction of American D-Boy Records. That's the end goal." John looked up at the evening sky and took a deep breath. "I just want my life back."

"I agree, I feel like this is all my fault. If I wouldn't have started selling drugs like my life depended on it, then Agent Heron would've found someone else to sell drugs for him! I'm tired of this shit! When you think it's over, they start fucking with you again!" D-Boy shed tears as he spoke. "Now they are fucking with American D-Boy Records, something I started but my brother built! He made American D-Boy what it is today, not me! But because of me Agent Heron is destroying our legacy!" D-Boy was fuming.

"This chess game isn't over, we're only halfway through. We have a lot of moves left before we except defeat. Just know, the fact that we're alive, says we're a few moves ahead of Agent

Heron. Don't give in yet, we got this." John gave D-Boy a hug. "It's going to be alright, little brother."

"I know, I just get overwhelmed sometimes." D-Boy didn't like showing weakness.

"You hungry? I know this nice Italian restaurant up the block," John offered.

"Yeah, why not? It's been seven years since I had real Italian food."

———

DIRTY REDD'S **HOUSE IN LONG ISLAND**

Sarah didn't like being pregnant. She thought about just terminating the baby every day and it had only been three months. She tried to get along with Dirty Redd, but it wasn't working. Every time he was near her she wanted to throw up, so she did. It was so bad they didn't even sleep in the same room. Good thing there were four other empty rooms in the house.

She became highly sexual, but she didn't want Dirty Redd. She thought about having sex with Special Agent Heron all day. They had a connection that was primal when it came to sex. They were into the same freaky things, so they had great sexual chemistry. The fact that they were both spies turned them on that much more. They were a match made in espionage heaven.

She tried not to call Agent Heron, but the sexual images in her head wouldn't allow her not to. "Hey, Agent Stud." She licked her lips. "I can't wait until this mission is over, so I can fuck the shit out of you! I can't stop thinking about the last time we fucked. You tied my ankles to my wrist while I bent over a barstool and pummeled my pussy," she reminisced.

"I can't stop thinking about it either. It turns me on to know you're fucking Dirty Redd. Is he fucking you right?" Agent Heron asked.

"Not like you. He doesn't beat me, choke me, or spit on me

like I beg you to do to me. He's a boring fuck compared to you!"
she complained.

"This mission is going to be over shortly, then we can have
all the fun we want," Agent Heron assured her.

"I can't wait to get away from him, he's so annoying. He
makes me want to throw up every time he's near me," Sarah said
with disgust.

"I got an idea, why don't you video chat with me while you
play with your pussycat," Agent Heron requested.

"Okay, let me take my jeans off and I'll Facetime you."
Sarah removed her tight jeans and called Agent Heron. "Hey,
you ready to have some fun?"

Agent Heron pulled his pants down around his ankles. "I am
now, let me see that pussy. It's been so long since I touched it."
Agent Heron stroked his penis.

"I see that cock, I miss deep throating it." Sarah touched her
clitoris. "Fuck yeah, I can't wait."

———

DIRTY REDD'S HOUSE, **DRIVEWAY**

Dirty Redd pulled up to the house and sat in his Bentley.
He was watching the new high-tech hidden surveillance
system he had secretly installed in his house. The way Sarah
was acting and moving suspiciously was the reason he did it.
Sarah had no idea she was being watched and heard at this
very moment. He was heartbroken from what he was
watching.

*"I can't wait to get away from him, he's so annoying. He
makes me want to throw up every time he's near me," Sarah said
with disgust.*

*"I got an idea, why don't you video chat with me while you
play with your pussycat."*

"Okay, let me take my jeans off and I'll Facetime you." The

man paused while she removed her jeans. "Hey, you ready to have some fun?"

He pulled his pants down around his ankles. "I am now, let me see that pussy. It's been so long since I touched it," he said as he stroked his penis.

"I see that cock, I miss deep throating it." Sarah touched her clitoris. "Fuck yeah, I can't wait."

"I bet you can't wait." Dirty Redd wiped the tears and looked at the video closer. "What the fuck?" He zoomed in on her phone so he could see the screen clearer. "The Central Intelligence Agency!" He turned it off. He couldn't watch anymore. "Who the fuck is this bitch?"

Dirty Redd wasn't sure what to do, call Mouf or Jay-Roc. "Fuck it I'll call them both." He called Mouf first. "Yo Mouf, hold on I'm getting Jay-Roc on the conference call." He put Mouf on hold and called Jay-Roc, "Okay, you both there?" he asked.

"Yeah, I'm here what's going on?" Jay-Roc asked in a confused tone.

"Word, what the fuck you got going on, Dirty?" Mouf asked.

"Listen, I think Sarah is down with the Central Intelligence Agency," Dirty Redd whispered as if he wasn't alone. "I saw a video of her talking to a dude that had the CIA logo in the background. They were talking about Sarah ending her mission and stuff like that."

Before anyone could say another word Jay-Roc spoke, "Listen to me very carefully, do not approach her about what you know. Both of you are meeting me tomorrow afternoon at the office and I'll discuss some things with you. Make sure you don't say anything to anyone about this, understood?" Jay-Roc never showed them this side of him, so they knew this was very serious.

"I got you big dog," Dirty Redd replied. "I'm going to act like nothing ever happened."

"Yeah right! We know you can't hold water, Dirty," Mouf said.

"For real, I know this is serious when the CIA is involved," Dirty Redd responded.

"See you tomorrow. Twelve noon sharp." Jay-Roc hung up and called D-Boy. "We have a problem."

"What's popping?" D-Boy asked.

"Sarah is an agent for the CIA, most likely she's working with Agent Heron. Meet me at the office at twelve noon." Jay-Roc hung up.

D-Boy looked at John. "You were right, Sarah is an agent."

John smiled. "That's nice to know."

CHAPTER 14
AMERICAN D-BOY
RECORDS

Everyone showed up at the same time. They quietly moved as if they were under surveillance. Single file they entered the conference room and took a seat. A lot had to be explained to Dirty Redd and Mouf, they inadvertently fell into some proverbial 'shit.'

John already had a master plan; his only issue was with Dirty Redd and Mouf. He wasn't sure they were built for this or if they could hold water. Just because people presented themselves as being 'real,' everyone would be held accountable for what they are. Now was the moment of truth for Dirty Redd and Mouf.

John stood up and directed his attention to Dirty Redd and Mouf. "I greet you in my language, Shabbat Shalom. I have a lot to explain and very little time to do it. My name is John Gillespie, I was a prominent Attorney here in New York City. I represented Darius 'D-Boy' Jensen, who you probably have heard of in the streets. D-Boy didn't have a case, he retained me for the future. I did background checks on his supplier and discovered George Heron was a Special Agent for the Central Intelligence Agency conducting a rogue drug operation. I knew their endgame, sending D-Boy to prison for life or killing him. I wasn't going to let either happen to my client, who became my friend. They found out I was snooping into them, so I knew they were going to kill us both. I devised a plan for D-Boy and I to fake our deaths and move to Dubai for seven years until any investigating is done. You met us in Dubai as Mustafa and Rahman." He paused to see if they were up to speed. They both just looked at each other with the same facial expression of bewilderment.

"Now I'm going to explain Sarah's involvement. Agent Heron deployed Sarah on a mission to get intel on Jay-Roc's activities to see if there was any chance we were alive and where we were hiding. Agent Heron doesn't have the full support of the agency, so he's limited in what he can do. My presumption is that Agent Heron is getting desperate because he knows if word gets out that he's conducting an independent drug operation using the agency network, he's fried. We also know that Agent Heron's hands are in the making of the rapper YC. The CIA controls the entertainment business so it's easy for them to super-impose a new artist on people in ways that are invisible to the naked eye. This is an effort to destroy American D-Boy Records and flush us out of hiding. I need both of you to keep this to yourselves and assist us by acting normal around Sarah. We want her to report the info we design for her to keep Agent Heron relaxed, so he won't see it coming." John ended his speech and sat down as if he was talking about the weather.

"Wow," Mouf said. "That was some real spy, espionage double cross shit!"

"Word! I learned my lesson about quickly falling for chicks. This shit crazy!" Dirty Redd was still in disbelief about Sarah.

"I'm going to need you two to lay low on this matter. You can't say a word about this, it can get you killed. The agency leaves no loose ends, if they find out you know about any of this they'll murder you." John looked at Mouf and Dirty Redd. "Understood?"

"Hell yeah, I'm not trying to fuck with the CIA," Mouf responded.

"Me either, even though I fuck with one, but you know what I mean," Dirty Redd added.

"You are dismissed," John said in order that they leave.

"I'll see you at the show tonight," Mouf said while he was exiting.

"I almost forgot we had a show tonight," Dirty Redd said.

"You would forget your head if it wasn't attached to your neck," Jay-Roc said playfully.

When they were gone, John spoke, "Now I know for sure that Sarah killed Prime. I didn't want to mention it around Mouf and Dirty Redd because it would've caused too many emotions and Dirty Redd would've blown our cover. We'll just keep that between us until this blows over."

"I agree, I didn't even want to tell them about D-Boy. You think you know someone until they show you who they really are," Jay-Roc said.

"They have more to lose by speaking on it. If my plan works we'll be exonerated by Senator Green from the Oversight Committee. That's our one shot at redemption." John looked at Jay-Roc and D-Boy in their eyes.

"Let's get to it! Let us know the next move." D-Boy was anxious to get his freedom back.

"We need to contact YC. If we can get him to understand what he's gotten himself into and switch sides, we can use him as leverage," John explained.

"Let's plan a trip to ATL! I can get to him and convince him to ride with us," D-Boy offered.

"Okay, if you think you can handle it without causing him to blow it up, by all means be my guest," John replied.

"Say less, just show me a picture of him and give me some basic intelligence. I'll be on the next thing smoking," D-Boy said.

"Okay, I'll have the information you requested in two days, meanwhile Jay-Roc keep a tight leash on Mouf and Dirty Redd. Keep them close to you for a while until this is over. I'm counting on you," John said to Jay-Roc.

"I got you, John, I need to be close to them anyway. I need to inspire some magic so they can record some new fire!" Jay-Roc proposed.

"Okay, then it's settled. D-Boy you got YC in Atlanta, Jay-Roc you got Mouf and Dirty Redd, and I got Senator Green. Fellows we can't have no screw ups, let's get our lives back once and for all." D-Boy nodded in agreement with John's statement.

"I'm ready!" D-Boy said with vigor.

SOUTHSIDE OF ATLANTA

Fernando and Diego met a couple of Lost Souls defectors, Carlos and Ray. They were illegals that made a life transporting from Texas to all parts of the US. Carlos and Ray had access to ten heavy weight customers that would take the 100 kilos ASAP. They were going to need more to supply the ten customers, but this was a good start for Fernando and Diego's new cartel.

The four of them agreed that being members of the Lost Souls Cartel wasn't working out. King Cobra wanted total control over his soldiers. He expected you to put his life over your own. The horrific stories of King Cobra relentlessly killing his own men is what made most men defect.

"My shipment should be here this week, then we can transport my work to your people," Fernando said to Carlos and Ray. "And I'm promising you a bigger cut than you were getting."

"Hey, I'm all in, brother." Carlos clinked his beer mug into Fernando's in a cheer.

"What about some customers from Atlanta?" Diego asked.

"We used to serve this crew, but they stopped fucking with us all of a sudden. Then I see this guy all over the TV, he's a rapper, they call him YC. Looks like he made it big rapping, so he gave the game up," Ray replied.

"That's what we need, a gang that needs a plug. We can blow them up at the same time, getting richer quicker. My uncle, Diaz, always told me to work smarter not harder," Fernando stated.

"I agree, but hey, if your work is good we can take all the customers," Carlos said.

"We got the best product out, hands down. It's all about how you treat the soil that you grow from, and not using kerosine to extract the coke from the leaves. I have a secret formula that makes my cocaine come out so pure, you can step on it five times and it's still the best out," Fernando bragged about his product.

"I hear what you're saying, I have to see it to believe it. When will it be here?" Ray asked.

"It was supposed to be here last week. I'm hoping it didn't get caught at customs. I haven't heard from my cousin in five days," Fernando said nervously.

"That's not a good sign, brother. Let's just hope everything is okay," Carlos added.

At that moment, Fernando's phone rang. It was his cousin. "Bro', I lost my phone and I had to buy a new one, but I'm here at the address with the work. Where the fuck you at?"

Fernando smiled. "Speaking of the devil, I was just talking about you. I'm up the street at this bar with some ex-Lost soul members. I'll see you in ten minutes, don't pay the old lady any attention. Just tell her you're my cousin from Columbia."

When they got there Milly had already gotten to his cousin Pedro. "Let me tell you something, if Fernando isn't here in five minutes you have to get the fuck off my property. This isn't no stop and stay, get your taco eating ass the fuck out of here!" Milly was going off on a drunken tirade when Fernando arrived.

"I'm sorry, Milly, my cousin Pedro was waiting on me to

come back from the bar," Fernando said while escorting Pedro to the apartment door with the work.

"If you didn't get here, I was going to toss his ass on the sidewalk myself." Milly walked inside her apartment and closed the door.

Fernando, Diego, Carlos, Ray, and Pedro all piled into the small apartment. Fernando couldn't wait to open one of the kilos so he could have Carlos test it for purity. Fernando was just bragging about the potency of his product, now was the moment he'd been waiting for.

"Now we can see if this shit is as good as you say it is." Carlos rubbed his hands together.

Fernando took out one of the bricks of cocaine and opened it enough to take out a pinch for Carlos to rub on his gums. Carlos took the small amount and rubbed it on his gums. Within seconds the powerful substance took effect. His jaws locked up and he couldn't speak. Fernando watched him as he tried to speak but nothing came out.

"This shit is too fucking raw!" Carlos was able to say after sampling Fernando's product.

"Now do you believe me? My secret formula will make us not only wealthy, but we'll be the most powerful cartel on earth!" Fernando was confident in his work.

"You can probably turn one brick into four and this will still be the best coke in the United States! I've been a drug chemist for twenty years and I can honestly say, you're a fucking genius!" Carlos shook his hand. "I'm all in, let's do this!"

"Count me in!" Ray shook Fernando's hand as a sign of allegiance.

"Here's the plan, we need an army. Here in America gangs are plentiful, so we'll target all of the gangs first. That's how we'll amass thousands of workers and a strong team because we'll recruit only the bosses of these gangs. We'll let the gang's leaders control their men, we'll just control the leaders of all the gangs through my product. This is exclusive so we're going to charge more, they can't get it anywhere else but from us," Fernando explained.

"You're going to change the game with this. People are going to only want your product once they get a taste," Carlos said.

"I heard you say that you're a drug chemist. That's exactly what I need. Can you create a cut that won't decrease the integrity of the product? I don't want the basic B-12 or lactose, I need something that acts as a binding agent," Fernando explained.

"I got exactly what you need, it's a derivative of the coffee plant. When you mix caffeine with cocaine you get a whole different high. If we mix it with what you got, we're talking about a different drug altogether. We can call it something different, to market it as the new cocaine," Carlos said.

"I like that, you're onto something. Get as much of that cut as you can and let's get to work so we can get this money!" Fernando was excited about his new venture with Carlos and Ray.

They used Carlos's new cut and just like he predicted they created a whole new experience. It was like no high. It was clean and didn't leave any horrible side effects. It sped up your thoughts to the point that Carlos swore it was making him smarter.

"I could think so fast that I was multi-thinking if that makes sense. Then I was able to execute my thoughts in real time. It was incredible!" Carlos was officially the guinea pig because no one else was bold enough to try it first.

"Fuck it, here goes nothing." Fernando took a healthy snort of the new concoction. In five seconds his mind was racing. "Yo! I see what you were saying. I can't stop thinking, I just had ten great ideas in ten seconds and it won't stop!" Fernando was amazed at the way it was making him feel so he took more. "This shit is a wonder-drug, it's making me smart."

After they cut all 100 kilos they had 400 kilos of their new Super-Coke, that was the name they settled on. They didn't want to market it as a different drug, just a better version of the original. They started off by transporting 100 kilos to Carlos's customers in New York. In five days they were demanding 100 more. They met a connect from the West Coast that took fifty kilos. In three days he wanted to purchase 150 kilos of Super-Coke.

They met up with gang members in Atlanta. One of them was a short chubby guy named Butta. He was YC's new second in command since Cheese's untimely demise. When Butta got his hands on Super-Coke it was over, he swore that it was the end for regular coke. Much like that marijuana game, when the Super-Gas came out it was over for regular weed. This was the end of doing regular coke, Super-Coke was the new coke of choice.

"I'm trying to tell you, this Super-Coke lives up to its name. This shit is like coke on steroids without the side effects. It's what everyone is asking for," Butta said to YC with excitement.

"Where did this shit come from?" YC asked with curiosity.

"I don't know exactly, but I heard its some amigos from Columbia that's making it. It's a secret formula, it's coke though," Butta answered to the best of his knowledge.

"Find out who's making it and I'll make them an offer they can't refuse," YC said.

"What about the deal we made with Haitian John? We got loads of coke left from his people," Butta reminded YC of his deal.

"Fuck that nigga! If people want Super-Coke then that's what we're selling. Besides something don't sit right with me about Haitian John. I can't put my finger on it, it's just a hunch. Anyway, I'll deal with him, you just find the source of this Super-Coke and report back to me." YC knew this new Super-Coke was the wave, he wasn't going to miss it.

"I got you, big dog." Butta was close to the source, but he didn't know it. Butta delt with Carlos but didn't know he was part of the team pushing Super-Coke.

"What's good, boy? I was just talking about you," Carlos said when he answered the phone for Butta.

"I don't know, you got me some of that new Super-Coke everybody talking about?" Butta asked.

"Can I get it for you? I am half of the equation that made the shit! I can get you tons of Super-Coke!" Carlos was excited Butta was asking about Super-Coke because he wanted his gang as customers in Atlanta. They were running shit in the ATL, all Fernando needed was YC's gang and it was over.

"I need to connect you with YC. He runs shit in the ATL."

"Set it up, I'll bring my partner and we can negotiate a deal."

"We can meet at YC's condo in Buckhead later today. Is that cool?" Butta wanted to move on it fast.

"Sure, just send me the address."

"Bet!" Butta responded.

Fernando and Carlos went alone, they didn't need to bring the rest of the crew. Fernando wanted to get to know YC, he heard a lot about him. Fernando was a huge fan of rap culture, he grew up listening to American rap music since he was nine. He preferred listening to rap over his native Latin music.

"This guy YC is good!" Fernando listened to YC's music for the whole day.

"I heard. I don't like American rap music. It's trash!" Carlos replied harshly.

"We love rap in Columbia! It speaks to the struggle we all go through. I use to dream about being around American rappers one day and look I'm getting one as my customer," Fernando said with arrogance.

They pulled up to YC's building and rang the doorbell. "What it do?" YC said when he opened the door. "I'm the infamous YC." They shook hands before entering.

"It's a pleasure to meet you, YC, I'm a fan of your music," Fernando said.

"Come in, brother." YC ushered them into his luxury condo.

"Wow, this place is amazing!" Fernando said looking at the lavish condo.

"Good looking. That's the first thing I said when I came in here. I bought it furnished," YC explained.

They sat down. "Let's get down to business. Me and Fernando can get you as much Super-Coke as you need. We need something from you as well. Protection. You have the biggest gang in Atlanta, we need the assurance that you got our back, and we will supply you with all the Super-Coke you want," Carlos spoke to Fernando.

"That's nothing! I can give you twenty-four-hour security, no one will ever fuck with you. If they do it will be all out war!" YC assured them.

"Then we have a deal. How many kilos did you need?" Fernando asked YC.

"How many you got?" YC answered boldly.

Fernando looked at Carlos. "I was supposed to take 150 to California, but I'd rather sell them to you."

"I'll take them off your hands right now!" YC was eager to see what the craze was about this Super-Coke.

Fernando made a call to Diego. "Bring what we have left to the address I send you." Fernando hung up the phone and shook YC's hand. "It's done, your order will be delivered within the hour."

"I like that, my order will be delivered in one hour. This dude John is the middleman for someone. I can tell you are the boss of this operation, I can fuck with that." YC had respect for men like Fernando. "We're going to make a lot of money together, mi amigo."

CHAPTER 15
LOST SOULS COMPOUND, CALI, COLUMBIA

King Cobra was meeting with all of his top brass. Captain Diaz was front and center, and the subject of the discussion. Word spread fast about Captain Diaz's nephew Fernando and Diego's coup against the Lost Souls Cartel. Super-Coke is the number one drug of choice, not only in America but it was picking up steam in other countries.

Every cartel that exists was suffering from the instant popularity of Super-Coke. People were clamoring to feel the effects of Super-Coke, anyone that used it swore on a stack of Bibles it was the best high ever. Fernando had to increase his production tenfold, and that's when King Cobra got word of where his production facility was.

"You mean to tell me you knew nothing about your nephew's plans?" King Cobra was fuming.

"No sir. If I knew I would have stopped him in his tracks myself." Captain Diaz was one of the last loyal soldiers King Cobra could trust.

"I find that hard to believe because he lived with you. He did everything you advised him to do. Now you want me to believe you aren't in on this! Take him to the torture chamber. We'll see exactly what you know." Two men grabbed an arm and forcibly walked Captain Diaz toward his fate.

"Your Excellency, please don't do this! I swear I knew nothing about Fernando's plans! Please!" Captain Diaz's pleas fell on deaf ears as he was dragged away.

King Cobra turned to the rest of the men standing in attendance. "And that goes for anyone of you that think you can get away with crossing King Cobra!" He often spoke of himself in third person. "You are dismissed!"

All the men exited the room except Rodolfo. "I don't think it's wise to punish Captain Diaz. He is your most trusted soldier. He's been loyal to you forever. Fernando was always a strong-minded man. I truly don't think Diaz is a trader," Rodolfo pleaded for Captain Diaz.

"I have to make an example, so the men will know to never cross King Cobra," King Cobra said defiantly.

"I think if you were to torture Captain Diaz you will lose more men. You've had more than 100 soldiers leave Lost Souls, and word is that they left to join Fernando. The morale of the remaining men is low. If you hurt your top captain you will lose more than you think," Rodolfo advised.

"Maybe you're right. Go stop the execution!" King Cobra abruptly ordered.

"Yes sir." Rodolfo ran as fast as he could to the torture area. When he got there, Captain Diaz was still alive, but he was bleeding out. He was hanging from his wrist. "Get him down! King Cobra told me to stop the execution!"

The men quickly cut him down. He fell to the floor with a thud. Rodolfo knew it was too late, the old man was slowly dying. Rodolfo shed tears as he watched the innocent old man die from something he had no knowledge of. This was one of the main reasons soldiers were defecting from Lost Souls. The leader was a tyrant.

"I'm sorry this is happening to you, Captain Diaz." Rodolfo held him while he gasped for air.

"I dedicated my life to the Lost Souls Cartel, I would die before I betrayed King Cobra." Captain Diaz took his last breath, and his body went limp.

Rodolfo wept for the fallen soldier. "Rest in peace, soldier. You didn't die in vain, I promise you." Rodolfo was tired of pretending, he felt the same way Fernando felt.

King Cobra entered the torture chamber and saw Rodolfo holding Captain Diaz's dead body. "I guess you weren't fast enough to stop it, oh well." He spat on the ground and returned to the main section of the compound.

"You're going to pay for this!" Rodolfo said with vengeance.

———

FERNANDO'S NEW MANSION, SANDY SPRINGS, GA.

Fernando was swimming in cash. He made $14 million from his first flip. He spent $2 million cash for a 10K square foot mansion with ten bedrooms, ten bathrooms, a pool, sauna, workout room, and movie room. It was located in Sandy Springs, Georgia, a posh neighborhood thirty minutes from the hell hole on the southside.

He bought five Mercedes Benz's, all different models, one for himself and the other four for Diego, Carlos, Pedro, and Ray. Those were the top four trusted men of his new organization. He made sure they were good at all times. He didn't want to make the mistake King Cobra made, keeping all of the spoils for yourself.

He put his cousin, Pedro, in charge of transporting, which was the hardest job. They were able to get another 100 kilos of coke to be mixed into Super-Coke. That wasn't nearly enough to meet the demand. They needed a ton, and that would last three months. They had the drug game on lock down.

Fernando knew he had to come up with a better way to ship his product to America. Bringing 100 kilos at a time wasn't cutting it, he needed a plane or a large boat to get his product shipped to the US. He didn't know anyone personally that had those capabilities. For now he had to get it in the best way possible, which was the method Pedro was using. It was slower and he could only carry 100 kilograms at a time.

"Who do we have to pay to bring in a thousand bricks?" Fernando was asking YC. "I know you know someone that knows someone that can bring more of the work in."

"You know something, I may know someone that can assist us. My old connect, Haitian John, he has to know someone that is bringing in more than 100 bricks at a time. He has dumped about 500 bricks on me, I got about 300 of them bitches left. I stopped selling his shit once I started selling Super-Coke," YC explained.

"See what you can find out. Tell him a got $250K for him if he can give me a plug to get a ton shipped from Columbia." Fernando was desperate.

"I got you, even though I've been ducking him for a month because he's been trying to dump more on me. That's why I said he must be growing it," YC replied.

"I'm curious, did your bricks come with a stamp on it?" Fernando asked.

"Yeah, it did, it was a snake, you know of those whatchacallit —" YC was at a loss for words.

"A red King Cobra?" Fernando added.

"Yeah, how did you know it was red?" YC was curious now.

"He's getting it from the Lost Souls drug cartel, I used to be a soldier for them. Anyone dealing with King Cobra is high up on the food chain. See what you can find out." Fernando shook his hand. "If you'll excuse me I have to prepare your order, as you know it'll be delivered within the hour."

"My man! I'll see you later, and I got you on that plug. One hand washes the other, they both wash the face, you feel me?" YC exited the mansion and skated away in his royal blue Rolls Royce Wraith.

As Fernando strolled through the mansion, he walked pass Diego speaking on the phone. It caught his attention because he rarely saw Diego get emotional about anything. Whatever was being said was tragic because Diego suddenly started crying uncontrollably, another trait Diego seldom showed.

"I'll tell him," Diego said before hanging up,

"Tell me what?" Fernando knew Diego was speaking of him.

Diego couldn't control the stream of tears. "Uncle Diaz, he's... he's dead."

"How? Who did this to my uncle?" Fernando was shocked and hurt at the same time.

"They said King Cobra had him killed because he accused Uncle Diaz of being a part of our moves to start our own cartel. He didn't believe Diaz when he swore his allegiance to Lost Souls was greater than his allegiance to his own flesh and blood. So he had him tortured to death," Diego spoke through a river of tears.

Fernando turned away from Diego before he let out a heart-breaking sound and broke down to his knees sobbing. "Why God? Uncle Diaz was the most loyal man. He loved the ground that demon King Cobra walked on. You didn't have to kill him! You know he loved you!" Fernando shouted with pure venom.

Diego helped Fernando to his feet. "Come on brother, we need you to be strong. Uncle Diaz would want you to be strong." Diego's words sparked something in Fernando.

He dried his tears and cracked his neck by turning it side to side. "You're right, Diego. He wants us both to be strong. That's why from this day forward you and I will be known as the Diaz

Brothers, and we operate the Diaz Cartel!" Until today Fernando couldn't come up with a name for his organization.

"The Diaz Cartel!" Diego shouted.

"Our sworn enemy is King Cobra and his Lost Souls Cartel. I won't rest until I crush everything he has ever loved. It's war!" Fernando had the money and the power with his Super-Coke, now he had respect with the gang behind him.

―――――

CIA HEADQUARTERS, **LANGLEY, VIRGINIA**

Things were falling apart for Special Agent Heron. He was stuck with a ton of coke that he couldn't move because of Super-Coke. The new drug of choice was Super-Coke and if you didn't have it you weren't getting money. YC stopped taking bricks from Haitian John which was only hurting Special Agent Heron's pockets.

"What the fuck do you mean he isn't fucking with you?" Heron asked Haitian John.

"YC isn't taking my phone calls or calling back. He moved so I don't know where he is to even try to talk to him. He ghosted me," Haitian John responded.

"You better find him or you're going to find yourself in a fucking jail cell for life!" Special Agent Heron hung up the phone and faced Director Cohen, who was sitting in a chair looking at Heron with disgust.

"You mean to tell me that our asset is missing!" Director Cohen shouted.

"I can explain," Heron attempted to speak but was abruptly cut off.

"I don't want to hear any of your excuses. We can't send any agents into the field on this mission. No mistakes can be made, the agency can't know anything about this so we're on our own. This is why I'm concerned. Tell me about this Super-

Coke that's trending on the market," Director Cohen asked curiously.

"It's like nothing I've ever seen before, not since we put crack in the Black neighborhoods. It's cocaine on steroids, and it's taking the place of regular coke. Everyone wants Super-Coke," Agent Heron explained.

"Who is making this Super-Coke?"

"We don't know yet, but our intelligence is pointing toward a defector of the Lost Souls Cartel."

"Find him! Get the formula and dispose of him! This Super-Coke is throwing a monkey wrench in my partnership with Gill Bates. I want this defector found immediately!" Director Cohen stood up and left the office.

"Yes sir," Agent Heron spoke to Cohen's backside as the door slammed behind him.

Special Agent Heron knew he was expendable if he didn't fix this problem. Director Cohen didn't tolerate mistakes, especially mistakes that cost millions of dollars. Being that this was a rogue operation there was little support they could get without tripping suspicion. This operation was getting too dangerous for Agent Heron. He wanted to terminate it, but he couldn't because Director Cohen had other interests involved at the highest level.

CHAPTER 16
SENATOR GREEN'S OFFICE, WASHINGTON, DC

Senator Green was reviewing the information presented to him by an anonymous whistleblower. It claimed that top officials at the CIA were running a rogue drug operation using American citizens to unknowingly commit crimes that benefited the operatives. It was a scathing report on how the CIA created a pipeline that transported heroin from Afghanistan to the United States. Once the heroin was in the US, they would hand it directly to a dealer to sell it for them.

The whistleblower was speaking on behalf of John and D-Boy. "He has pictures, visual and audio of money transactions, the works. He has enough evidence to bury the CIA once and for all."

Senator Green clasped his hands together before speaking. "This is no surprise to me. You know, President Kennedy warned us about organizations like the CIA and the FBI. He referred to them as 'repugnant.' He was right, they've mettled in the affairs of countries serving only themselves and their wicked satanic agendas, under the guise that they are working for the American people." Senator Green was very concerned about these allegations.

"I know all too well. I used to be an agent for the CIA for

twenty years so I know about the coups we created that toppled governments around the world. Good men that believed in democracy were replaced with agents that exploited the country into poverty. This is why it's important to me that my friends are exonerated for all known and unknown crimes committed for the agency. They want full protection of the United States government against the tyranny of the CIA." The whistleblower known as K was passionate about helping John and D-Boy get back their freedom.

"You do understand that no one is safe from the CIA, not even a standing United States Senator. They have a history of being murderous against anyone that opposes them. This is not going to be an easy battle. They've been challenged in the past and they always came out victorious. We have to be very secretive about this, no one can know what we're planning until the day it's presented to the Oversight Committee." Senator Green knew how dangerous exposing the CIA was.

"I understand, just let me know when you want to present the information and I'll have all the evidence for you at that time. Not a second before or after. When you're ready you know how to call me." The whistleblower stood up and shook the Senator's hand. "Thank you for your service to the American people." He exited the office.

When K left the Senator's office he didn't notice the janitor in the hallway. He was an agent keeping tabs on Senator Green. Senator Green was on the list of politicians the agency couldn't bribe so he was a threat.

The agency knew about his meetings concerning their covert activities. He'd been speaking candidly about how no organization should have so much power they can present information that starts a war. The information could be fake, a lie, and cost thousands of American lives.

"Follow the guy with the blue New York Yankee hat, he's

coming out of the front door now," the agent spoke to the mic hidden in the collar of his shirt.

K was no amateur, right before he went through the revolving door he switched his hat inside out and it was a red Cincinnati hat. He walked right past the agents that were looking for him to come out with a Blue New York Yankees hat on. K knew how the agency worked, he knew they had tabs on Senator Green for the things he was saying.

K walked a block before calling John. "It's done, I just made contact with Senator Green. Now all we have to do is wait on the hearing date to present the evidence."

"Copy, thank you, K," John responded.

"Don't mention it." K hung up.

John looked at D-Boy and sat back in his reclining chair. "Next three moves is checkmate. When you get to Atlanta and make contact with YC to persuade him to become our ally that will be our second move. The revenue coming from American D-Boy Records is the only income we have. YC's attack is killing us."

"I'm on it, I used to recruit young cats for my organization all the time. This is a piece of cake, or shall I say peach cobbler," D-Boy added sarcastically.

"Let's hope so, our lives depend on it," John specified the seriousness of their mission.

"My fight to ATL is tomorrow morning, and oh yeah, in order for me to win him over I can't go looking like no lame. I'm going all out to make a statement. Roll with us or get rolled over," D-Boy declared defiantly.

"Of course. Go all out as you call it, just get the job done," John replied in a stern tone.

"ATL! Get ready for D-Boy!"

CHAPTER 17
HARTSFIELD-JACKSON ATLANTA INTERNATIONAL AIRPORT

D-Boy landed at eleven a.m. right before noon. He looked up all the popular spots to hang out, he was going to have as much fun as possible while he was in Atlanta. D-Boy didn't really get a chance to have fun when he returned to the states, now was his time to shine.

He rented a Rolls Royce Ghost and stayed at the Westin because it was right next door to Lenox Square mall and everything he wanted to do. D-Boy bought a suitcase with little in it, just a couple pairs of boxer shorts and tee-shirts. He planned on going shopping at all of the expensive designer brands they had available at Lenox and Phipps Plaza across the street.

D-Boy did his research. He was very interested in the culture of Atlanta. He read that Atlanta had more Black owned businesses per capita than anywhere on the planet. This fact piqued his curiosity, so he did more digging.

He read about Sweet Auburn, which was a wealthy Black community built in 1865. It was the center for Black cultural, spiritual, and economic prosperity in a time when Blacks were undergoing extreme oppression. It was known for producing Black excellence. One of Sweet Auburn's most notable facts was it was the birthplace of the civil rights icon, Dr. Martin Luther King.

As he was researching, he discovered he would be in Atlanta for the 'Sweet Auburn Festival,' so he put that on his schedule of things to do. The first thing on his list was making contact with YC. It had to feel organic, not fake or forced.

He did some background on YC, which was easy because he was the hottest new rapper out. He was raised by his father, who was a major drug dealer. He adapted to the streets because of the way his father raised him.

He was on fire, to the point that he singlehandedly took on the Billigoats. Dirty Lo was forgotten once the fans heard YC. They liked him more than Dirty Lo. The sales told the truth that the people's choice was YC. Even though YC's music was secretly being pushed ahead of everything else, the fact that he was real increased his likability. YC was the new 'it' guy.

"My daddy taught me to have no fear, and to never be afraid to get money. I'm a risk taker because I learned if you don't try it yourself you'll never know the true outcome, ya feel me?" YC spoke like a true soldier in the interview D-Boy watched on his phone.

After watching a few of YC's interviews he had a newfound respect for him. *Me and YC have more in common than I thought. He was raised by a gangster father and so was I. We were both reared by the streets. I can relate to him, I understand his mind-set. I know how to get to him, just be myself.*

D-Boy was posing as a bigtime club promoter named Blast. He secured a meeting with YC's label head, G-Mack, to negotiate a deal to book YC for four shows at $100K a piece. YC will be at the meeting and that's where he planned to strike up a conversation to get YC to switch sides on Agent Heron. What D-Boy didn't know was that YC had already started the process by ignoring Haitian John and dealing exclusively with the Diaz Brothers.

In the meantime D-Boy had time to kill. He went shopping at Christian Dior and Louis Vuitton, and then he got something to eat at NOBU. He went back to the Westin to get dressed and to go over his role. He turned on the radio to V103. DJ Greg Street was on the air.

"Don't forget this weekend is the annual Sweet Auburn Festival, it'll be food venders, independent Black businesses, the works! Make sure you make it down there, you won't regret it. Coming up next we got the new joint from that boy YC. Stay tuned, it's your boy Greg Streets and you're listening to V-103!"

"A new joint from YC, let's hear what he's talking about." D-Boy waited for the new song to play. "That was actually dope! The more I listen to this cat, the more I like him."

He finished getting dressed and put the address in his GPS. The location was thirty minutes away. He jumped in the ghost and drove slowly, taking in the scenery of Atlanta. He was liking the vibration he was getting. It was like New York but just a bit slowed down. He liked the pace. It wasn't too slow, it was just right for D-Boy. He wanted a change of pace anyway, New York changed a lot in seven years.

When he got to Get Money Records there was a group of thugs hanging in the parking lot. They all stopped talking to watch the Rolls Royce Ghost slide into a parking spot. They wanted to see who it was. It wasn't every day that a newcomer pulls up in a $300 thousand car.

"Who the fuck that nigga?" one of them asked.

"I don't know but he looks like money to me." The second guy showed his weapon as if he was going to rob D-Boy.

"Don't do that, G-Mack gave us specific instructions not to do fuck shit on his property," the first guy replied.

D-Boy strolled to the front door and rang it, G-Mack opened the door in seconds. "What up? Are you Blast?"

"Yeah, in the flesh," D-Boy answered.

"Come this way, YC been waiting on you." G-Mack led him

through a hallway to his office where YC was sitting. "YC, this is Blast, the promoter I was telling you about."

YC stood up and shook D-Boy's hand. "Nice to meet you, Blast."

"The pleasure is all mine, I'm a huge fan! That's why I'm here. I want to get some money with you, while the getting is good," D-Boy said in his signature New York accent.

"You from New York?" YC asked.

"Southside Jamaica Queens! Right up the block from where 50 Cent grew up." D-Boy loved his hood.

"That's what's up, I fuck with New York niggas," YC said.

"We fuck with ATL niggas. All they play on the radio in New York is Atlanta music. You would think you're in ATL," D-Boy explained.

"I heard. G-Mack told me I stream more in New York than anywhere in the North." YC was proud to know the love he received from New York.

"Let's get down to business, we can talk about New York later," G-Mack interrupted the conversation.

"It's simple, I'm trying to get a deal on booking YC. I know he's getting $100K for a twenty-minute show. I got $400K for five shows if I pay up front," D-Boy proposed.

"Okay, so you want the fifth show on the arm." G-Mack shook his head up and down while he thought. "And you said you're paying the whole $400K up front and not half up front like usual." G-Mack looked at YC. "What you think?"

"Shit, if buddy is paying the whole thing up front I can do the fifth show included," YC agreed.

"You got a deal! How do you want your money, cash, Zelle, or cash app?" D-Boy asked.

"Cash is king!" YC replied.

"Cash it is! I can have it for you tomorrow."

A bell went off indicating someone was at the door. "It's John, let him in!" G-Mack shouted to someone in the front.

"Fucking John, I've been ducking him," YC said.

"I know, that's why I had him come here. You can't do him like that player, he's a major plug." G-Mack was in on the game.

"Fuck it, I'll see what he is talking about." YC didn't want to deal with John because the Super-Coke was doing numbers.

Haitian John entered the office and greeted G-Mack first, "What's up my nigga?" They shook hands, then he turned to YC. "Big Dog! What's been up with you? I've been trying to dump this next load on you."

"I'm good on the work. I'm going to pay you for the work you gave me, but honestly I got a better connect." YC saw Haitian John's jaw drop.

"What do you mean? You going to fuck up a good thing," Haitian John sounded desperate because if he didn't fulfill his obligation to Special Agent Heron he was going to jail for life.

Haitian John was being rude, he didn't acknowledge D-Boy at first, but when he looked at him they both got the chills. They definitely knew of each other from a not-so-distant past. D-Boy got the same vibe, like he knew him, but he wasn't getting a good feeling from his intuition.

"What up they call me Blast," D-Boy broke the ice.

"They call me Haitian John, nice to meet you." When John stuck out his hand D-Boy saw the Haitian Mafia tattoo on the backside of his fist.

That's Haitian Amos crew's tattoo, I know this dude! He was Amos's bodyguard that Shoota shot the day he assassinated Amos for me. I thought the bodyguard died that day, I guess he lived, D-Boy thought before speaking.

D-Boy shook his hand and John looked at him one more time.

I know this fucking dude! This can't be, he's dead, but if I didn't know any better I would think he was fucking D-Boy, John thought.

The dark Versace shades D-Boy wore had kept his identity hidden this whole trip, but they weren't enough of a disguise for John not to notice him. D-Boy saw his wheels turning, it would only be a matter of time before he figured out that Blast was really D-Boy. "You good, my nigga? You look like you just saw a ghost," D-Boy said, trying to throw John off from his suspicion.

"You look just like this nigga from New York named D-Boy." Haitian John started inching his hand toward his waist where his 9-mm was.

D-Boy noticed his movements, and he didn't have a weapon. He thought back to the lessons John taught him in Dubai. *"It's one sweeping motion, don't force it,"* John said while demonstrating. *"See, it's a smooth motion, then you have the gun in your hand."*

Everything was moving in slow motion. Haitian John pulled out his weapon. "I know who the fuck you are!" he pulled out the 9-mm.

Here goes nothing, D-Boy thought before going into action.

D-Boy quickly grabbed the wrist that held the gun and twisted it hard and fast, causing him to drop the gun. But not before he let off a shot in the close quarter room. Everyone's ears started ringing from the loud gunshot. D-Boy swiftly picked up the gun.

"Yeah it's me motherfucker! I should murder your bitch ass!" Instead he pistol whipped him with his own gun until he was unconscious.

"What the fuck?" G-Mack said when D-Boy pointed the gun at him and YC.

"Put your guns on the floor nice and easy and kick them over to me." They both complied, took their guns out and kicked them over. "Good, now listen, I don't have any problems with you. My beef with him goes back eight years ago. He killed my girlfriend trying to kill me," D-Boy explained.

"I never like that motherfucker anyway. You cool with me," YC said.

G-Mack had different thoughts. "Who the fuck are you? You can't come in here pretending to be someone. Haitian John is my people." G-Mack knew him and Haitian John had to work together to stay free.

"Don't worry about who I am! Just know that the guy he's working for is the CIA and when they're done with you they will throw you away like trash." D-Boy tried to tell G-Mack something he already knew, but YC was oblivious.

"CIA! Wait a minute, who's CIA in this bitch! I don't fuck with no police. I knew this nigga wasn't right." YC didn't know the half.

D-Boy still had the gun pointed toward YC and G-Mack. "Listen, I have a lot to explain and very little time. YC you're in danger, the CIA has you in their sights, and they don't play fair, trust me."

"Don't listen to this dude! He came in here saying he was Blast, now he's someone else. You can see yourself out." G-Mack was pretending to not know anything about what D-Boy mentioned.

"You've been warned." D-Boy backed out of the office with the gun still pointed at them. When he got to his car he called John before he sped away from the scene. "Fuck! My cover is blown, Agent Heron is going to know we're alive. I fucked up!"

"Slow down, what happened?" John asked calmly.

"I was meeting with YC and G-Mack when this guy from my past came in the office. He spotted me and pulled out a gun. I unarmed him using the move you taught me in Dubai but he identified me, and I know he is working for Agent Heron," D-Boy spoke fast when he was upset.

"Get back to New York ASAP! You're not safe there, abort the mission." John hung up.

"So much for the Sweet Auburn Festival."

CHAPTER 18
DIRTY REDD'S HOUSE, LONG ISLAND, NEW YORK

Sarah loved to be in the house alone. She noticed Dirty Redd was being very distant to her lately. She liked it that way because she was having thoughts of killing him, the pregnancy was making her irritated and annoyed. She couldn't help it, her hormones were unbalanced so she'd rather be alone.

She was in the living room watching TV when she saw it. She thought she was seeing things. It was small and hidden in a good place. If she wasn't a trained agent she would've overlooked it. She walked up to it and pulled it out, and just like she thought, it was a hidden camera. She searched the whole house and found twenty hidden cameras and five listening devices.

"You sneaky bastard! You've been spying on me," she said to herself. "No wonder you've been so distant from me. What did you see or hear?" Sarah was nervous.

She waited for Dirty Redd to come home so she could go through his phone to see what he had on her. It all made sense to her now. He wasn't talking to her or trying to make up with her anymore. He let her have her attitude without responding, he just left the house every day until late at night.

Dirty Redd finally came home. Sarah was pretending to be sleeping when he entered the room and took his clothes off and got in the shower. He left his phone on top of the dresser, so she took the opportunity to look through it. It didn't take any time for her to find the video of her and Agent Heron having phone sex. As she looked she saw it as clear as day, the Central Intelligence Agency logo on the wall in the background.

"He knows." Her heart started beating hard and fast. She quickly called Agent Heron. "My cover is blown, I repeat my cover is blown, he knows."

"Get out of there ASAP! Abort the mission!" Agent Heron said with aggression.

Sarah didn't waste a second, she got dressed and called an Uber. The Uber was there within five minutes, she was gone before Dirty Redd got out of the shower. When Dirty Redd got out of the shower, he noticed his phone was playing the video of Sarah and Agent Heron.

"Fuck!" He looked around the house for Sarah. "Sarah!" When she didn't answer he knew she was gone. He called Jay-Roc. "She knows."

CHAPTER 19
K'S APARTMENT

K's APARTMENT WEST 116TH STREET & LENOX AVENUE. NEW YORK, NEW YORK

K got the call he'd been waiting on. "The Senator says you can come with all your evidence to Washington DC tomorrow. The Oversight Committee is secretly meeting about the CIA, so no one knows we're holding the meeting tomorrow."

"Thank you for the call, I'll be there bright and early tomorrow." K hung up and called John. "I just got the call, our hearing is tomorrow. It's secretive so the agency can't stop what they don't know."

"That's great news! Come to my spot immediately so we can go over the evidence." John was ecstatic. They finally had the chance to clear their names.

"I'll see you in thirty minutes." K hung up, quickly got dressed and left his apartment.

K lived on the ninth floor, and his elevator was very slow. He waited and it finally came. When he got on there was a man already on it. "How are you doing, sir?" K asked politely.

The man didn't speak, and he kept his head low. K found that strange, so he tried to get a good look at the man's face for his mental record. Call it a 'spy thing.' The man was avoiding eye

contact with K, again K found that peculiar, but he just carried
on and ignored him. That was until the man lifted his head and K
saw him clearly. It was the janitor from the hallway at Senator
Green's office.

The guy pulled out a 357 magnum with a silencer on it, but K
was swift. He pushed the barrel right before he let off a round.
They fought in the elevator for the gun. The janitor was stronger
than K, who was much older than the janitor. K gave up a good
fight but in the end the janitor got control of his weapon and shot
K twice in the head right before the elevator opened on the first
floor. There was no one standing there to get on, so he stepped
over K's body and exited the building. He was gone before
anyone could notice K's dead body lying on the elevator floor.

John waited for two hours before trying to call K. "Come on,
K, pick up the phone!"

After five more tries, John concluded that K was compromised, and he was probably dead. John and K were close, they
went back to the spy days together. Although K was an American spy, the Israeli spy agency, the Massad, interacted with the
CIA. They sometimes did operations together, that's how K and
John met. They'd been good friends ever since.

CHAPTER 20
CIA HEADQUARTERS.
LANGLEY, VIRGINIA

Sarah sat in Agent Heron's office waiting for Director Cohen to show up. She had to be debriefed before moving on. Her mission was over anyway because Haitian John confirmed that Darius 'D-Boy' Jensen was very much alive and well. Now all they had to do was recalibrate the plan.

Director Cohen opened the door and walked in the office very quietly. "Agent Sparrow, it's good to have you back with us. You did an amazing job, I'm proud of your ability. You're going to do well with the agency." Director Cohen smiled.

"Thank you, sir, I appreciate that coming from you," Sarah replied.

"Good day, sir," Agent Heron said while shaking the Director's hand. "I have some good news. We eliminated a major threat. A former agent named Kevin 'K' Gardner was seen at Senator Green's office. He was on his way to meet with John Gillespie, possibly to get the evidence he has on us. As of now the threat is neutralized, however the threat still exists so our job isn't done." There was a knock on the door. "Come in. This is Agent T, he's the agent that spotted K and eliminated him for us. He is going to be a member of our little team," Agent Heron explained.

"How are you guys doing?" Agent T, the janitor, was a big man.

"We can use a strong guy like T on our team. Did you brief him on the secrecy of our operation?" Director Cohen asked.

"Yes, he's fully aware of the risk," Agent Heron replied.

"So, for now D-Boy and John are neutralized. We can't put warrants out to apprehend them. The only remedy is to eliminate them, now that we know they are alive," Director Cohen ordered.

"They'll have to come up for air one day, and I'll be waiting. The other problem is our new D-Boy isn't cooperating. He's playing with another supplier, this Super-Coke is where the money is at. We need to align with the Diaz Brothers to solidify a deal with them to distribute their product," Agent Heron said.

"What about our deal with King Cobra and the Lost Souls Cartel?" Director Cohen asked.

"He's obsolete, his product is trash compared to the Diaz Brothers' Super-Coke. Besides sources tell me his cartel is folding, his soldiers are turning on him. It'll be a matter of time before they get rid of him," Agent Heron reported.

"Is there anything else?" Director Cohen asked while he walked toward the door, ready to exit the meeting.

"One more thing, Captain Miller is claiming the border is overrun with immigrants making this a national security issue. I'm thinking about dismissing him permanently because he knows too much," Agent Heron proposed.

"Yes, that's fine. He was a liability anyway." Cohen grabbed the doorknob. "Is that all?"

"That's all for now, Director Cohen," Agent Heron said as Director Cohen and Agent T exited the office.

Sarah looked at Agent Heron with sex in her eyes. "You ready?"

"You don't have to ask me twice!" Agent Heron pounced on her.

CHAPTER 21
AMERICAN D-BOY RECORDS

The team was all in attendance, D-Boy, John, Jay-Roc, Mouf, and Dirty Redd. This was like a locker room meeting after a team lost a championship game. They were defeated, but not broken. They still had hope at the end of the day because they still had freedom. With that they can live to see another day.

"When I came out of the shower my phone was playing the video I saved. Then she vanished, I haven't heard anything from her in four weeks. I don't even know if she kept the baby or not," Dirty Redd reported.

"That's fucked up, she left without telling you nothing about your baby. Bitches is trifling!" Mouf said feeling Dirty Redd's pain.

"They found my friend K's body in an elevator in his building. They got to him before he could meet with Senator Green again with the evidence. Our chances of getting back in front of the Senator are slim to none," John explained.

"That's fucked up! We were this close to winning our freedom back. Now what?" D-Boy asked.

"We come up with a better plan. We never surrender and never give up. As long as we have a life to live we have to fight.

It may look like they beat us, but that was just one round, there's ten more rounds to go. They may have won the battle, but they didn't win the war," John proclaimed.

"You right because it's not over 'til it's over! And I'm still standing!" D-Boy spoke with utter defiance.

ALSO BY BILLIGOAT

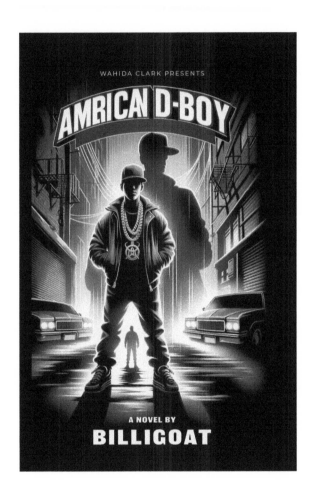